Seabreeze Inn and *Coral Cottage* series

"A wonderful story… Will make you feel like the sea breeze is streaming through your hair." – Laura Bradbury, Best-selling Author

"A novel that gives fans of romantic sagas a compelling voice to follow." – *Booklist*

"An entertaining beach read with multi-generational context and humor." – *InD'Tale* Magazine

"Wonderful characters and a sweet story." – Kellie Coates Gilbert, Bestselling Author

"A fun read that grabs you at the start." – Tina Sloan, Author and Award-Winning Actress

"Jan Moran is the queen of the epic romance." —Rebecca Forster, *USA Today* Bestselling Author

"The women are intelligent and strong. At the core is a strong, close-knit family." — Betty's Reviews

The Chocolatier

"A delicious novel, makes you long for chocolate." – *Ciao Tutti*

"Smoothly written...full of intrigue, love, secrets, and romance." – *Lekker Lezen*

The Winemakers

"Readers will devour this page-turner as the mystery and passions spin out." – *Library Journal*

"As she did in *Scent of Triumph*, Moran weaves knowledge of wine and winemaking into this intense family drama." – *Booklist*

The Perfumer: Scent of Triumph

"Heartbreaking, evocative, and inspiring, this book is a powerful journey." – Allison Pataki, *NYT* Bestselling Author of *The Accidental Empress*

"A sweeping saga of one woman's journey through World War II and her unwillingness to give up even when faced with the toughest challenges." — Anita Abriel, Author of *The Light After the War*

"A captivating tale of love, determination and reinvention." — Karen Marin, Givenchy Paris

BOOKS BY JAN MORAN

Coral Cottage Series

Coral Cottage

Coral Cafe

Coral Holiday

Coral Weddings

Coral Celebration

Coral Memories

A Very Coral Christmas

Summer Beach Series

Seabreeze Inn

Seabreeze Summer

Seabreeze Sunset

Seabreeze Christmas

Seabreeze Wedding

Seabreeze Book Club

Seabreeze Shores

Seabreeze Reunion

Seabreeze Honeymoon

Seabreeze Gala

Seabreeze Library

Crown Island Series

Beach View Lane

Sunshine Avenue

Orange Blossom Way

Hibiscus Heights

The Love, California Series

Flawless

Beauty Mark

Runway

Essence

Style

Sparkle

20th-Century Historical

Hepburn's Necklace

The Chocolatier

The Winemakers: A Novel of Wine and Secrets

The Perfumer: Scent of Triumph

Life is a Cabernet

JAN MORAN

A VERY *Coral* CHRISTMAS

A VERY CORAL CHRISTMAS

A NOVELLA

CORAL COTTAGE SERIES
BOOK 7

JAN MORAN

SUNNY PALMS
PRESS

Library of Congress Cataloging-in-Publication Data
Moran, Jan.
/ by Jan Moran

ISBN 978-1-64778-280-1 (ebook)
ISBN 978-1-64778-281-8 (paperback)
ISBN 978-1-64778-284-9 (audiobook)

Published by Sunny Palms Press. Cover design by Sleepy Fox Studios. Cover images copyright Deposit Photos.

Sunny Palms Press
9663 Santa Monica Blvd STE 1158
Beverly Hills, CA 90210 USA
www.JanMoran.com

1

*G*ingerbread cookies and cranberry bread were baking in the vintage O'Keefe & Merritt oven, filling Ginger's kitchen with the aromas of Christmas. Marina's grandmother had asked her to oversee the holiday food preparation this year.

"Peppermint hot cocoa, mulled cider, or mocha coffee—what's your pleasure?" Marina asked, turning to Jack.

Her husband grinned and leaned against the counter. Jack wore a silly Santa T-shirt, yet still managed to make it look good, with his bright blue eyes and thick hair that was a little longish. "How about an Irish coffee or a hot buttered rum?"

"I'm a chef, not a bartender. And you're incorrigible," she added, teasing him back.

"Yes, I am." Grabbing her apron strings, Jack pulled her closer. "Hold that thought until we get home. Have I told you how hot you look in that apron?"

Laughing, Marina sank into his arms, kissing her husband back with all the love in her heart like the newlyweds they still were. She'd missed this closeness for many years—especially during the holidays.

Just then, her grandmother breezed into her kitchen, wearing a cranberry-red cashmere sweater over a wool skirt with black riding boots. "I thought I might find you two hiding here like teenagers."

"I'm working," Marina replied, feigning innocence. "Jack's the instigator."

Oliver stood in the doorway behind Ginger and kissed her cheek. "I heard this is the kissing room."

"Not you, too," Ginger said with mock reproach.

Marina laughed at their antics, pleased that her grandmother's relationship with Oliver was developing. "I was planning the menu when Jack barged in looking for an Irish coffee."

Oliver's eyes brightened. "Put me down for one, too."

Ginger sliced a hand through the air. "Absolutely not. No alcohol until the decorations have been put up. There is no room for silly shenanigans while you're teetering on ladders, and I don't want to end the evening at the emergency room—especially with Chip's impressionable young sons. You must set an example for them."

Oliver kissed her other cheek. "You're a tough woman, Ginger Delavie. And you're right." He hooked his arms through hers. "Your elf volunteers are waiting outside for your orders. As am I," he added softly.

A special look passed between them, and Marina wondered what that was about. Still, she reined in her thoughts. Ginger and Oliver were entitled to their secrets and plans.

"You and Jack are in charge," Ginger said, her eyes

sparkling. "Use your creativity, and let's see what you can do."

"That could be dangerous." Jack put his hands on his hips. "But challenge accepted."

Marina glanced outside, appreciating the sunlit beach this time of year. "Your brothers-in-law are waiting for you."

Jack chuckled. "Axe and Chip hardly need a writer to help them with the heavy lifting."

Marina nudged him toward the door. "I'm sure you can hold your own with them." Brooke's husband Chip was a firefighter, and Kai's husband Axe was a general contractor, but Jack had been working out, too.

"Or Jack could chronicle the fiasco," Oliver said, laughing.

Jack motioned to the older man. "Let's strategize and supervise the others on the ladders. They can string the lights this year."

"I have full confidence you'll work it out," Ginger said. "I'll check on my helpers in the living room."

Everyone left, and Marina glanced from the window. In her grandmother's sunny yard, red bougainvillea, pink azaleas, and ivory roses were still in bloom, though beginning to wane with the cooler evenings.

Her sister Brooke had just helped Ginger plant a winter garden of lettuce, peas, broccoli, onions, and other root vegetables. Here in Southern California, they were lucky to garden most of the year.

After the sun set over the Pacific Ocean, a chill would fill the air, making it feel more like the holidays. Boots would replace flip-flops, and sweaters and jackets would be pulled over T-shirts. That's when her piping hot drinks would warm the family crew of helpers Ginger had organized.

Marina removed the gingerbread cookies from the oven and transferred them to cool on a rack. Quickly, she washed her mixing bowls to join her grandmother and the other half of the decorating crew.

Her daughter Heather sorted through boxes of decorations on the dining table. Her sister Brooke was also unpacking items while her baby, little Clover, sat in a playpen watching with wide eyes. On Ginger's orders, they all wore holiday colors for the photos they would take later. That was another tradition in the Delavie-Moore family.

"You still have more decorations in the garage," Heather said, brushing glitter from her hands onto her jeans. "Blake is getting those boxes for me."

"Good," Ginger said. "Let's pull out everything this year. What we don't use, and you girls don't want, we can give away. I have accumulated far too much over the years."

"Maybe we could sell some at the holiday market," Heather said. "Your vintage ornaments are beautiful. They'd fit right in."

Marina smiled at her daughter's entrepreneurial enthusiasm. This year, Marina's youngest sister, Kai, was helping manage a new holiday market extension to the farmers market. Locals were selling beautiful, handcrafted items.

"If you like them, they would be lovely on your tree after you and Blake marry." Ginger motioned to another carton. "Rather than selling anything, I prefer to donate items so other families can enjoy some holiday sparkle. That goes for anything else I no longer need or use."

Heather beamed. "I'd love that. Thank you."

Marina opened a box to reveal vintage ornaments she'd packed last year. "Do you want to keep these?"

Ginger peered over her shoulder with a fond sigh. "Bertrand and I collected those while we lived in Europe. They're beautiful, aren't they? Each one has a story."

"I'll take that as a yes." Marina began to unpack them.

She wasn't surprised at her grandmother's practicality. *I'm being sensible*, Ginger once told Marina when she appointed her as executor of her will. *I want to make the process easy for everyone whenever my time comes, and you're the most suited to the task.*

As she extracted the delicate ornaments, Marina chewed her lip. Was Ginger simply decluttering, or was there another reason behind her actions?

Then, considering how happy Ginger looked lately, Marina had another thought. *Perhaps she and Oliver are making plans for their future.*

She couldn't imagine Ginger giving up the Coral Cottage. Her husband Bertrand had given it to her as a wedding gift. Marina and her sisters had spent much of their lives here, especially after their parents died. Yet, she could understand Ginger's actions. Many of her grandmother's friends were downsizing or had moved to be close to their children.

Such was life, Marina knew. Still, Ginger was active, in excellent health, and even more vibrant with a new man in her life. Oliver wasn't exactly new, though; Ginger had known him for years. After his wife passed away and his brother Kurt reconnected them, their friendship evolved.

Ginger and Oliver were sweet together, and he was a welcome addition to the family. Still, there was more going on that Ginger had confided to her.

Behind her, a scream pierced the air, and Marina jerked her head up.

Kai stood in the doorway with little Stella, who wasn't quite a year old yet. Her sister looked perplexed, unable to soothe her. "I don't know what's suddenly gotten into her. Somebody, please help."

"My word," Ginger said after another earsplitting shriek hit a high note. "Stella has your voice, dear. Have you tried singing to her?"

"That usually works, but not this time," Kai said, raising her voice over Stella's. "When we walked through the door, she started her blood-curdling screams again."

"We noticed," Marina said, grinning.

Brooke reached for the squirming child. "I'll bet she wants to play with Clover." After placing her in the playpen with her little girl, Stella calmed down. The two cooed at each other as if admiring their similar outfits of red and green.

"Wow," Kai said, drawing her hands over her face in relief. "How did you know what to do?"

"I had plenty of practice with her brothers," Brooke replied. "They seem to have their own baby language. You'll learn to discern it."

Marina wiggled her fingers at her little nieces. Since they shared a birthday, she often bought them matching outfits. This time, she'd coordinated them with the same outfit in holiday colors. Their knit leggings were candy cane stripes, and their tops sported reindeer and snowflakes.

"They missed each other," Kai said, watching them. "Were we ever like that as kids?"

"Sort of." Marina shook a rattle at the girls, who

crawled to investigate. "You used to follow Brooke and me everywhere."

"And we hid from you," Brooke added with a guilty grin.

Kai crossed her arms with mild indignation. "All this time I thought we were playing hide-and-seek. I swear, the stories that come out during the holidays. Go figure."

Heather lifted a pair of wooden soldiers from a box. "Where do the nutcrackers go?"

"Let's have them flanking the fireplace this year," Ginger replied. "Not too close, of course. Place them on the other side of the Talavera pots."

While Heather positioned the hand painted nutcracker soldiers, Marina reached into a large carton and lifted out the wreath on top. Another one lay beneath it. She recalled making both with her sisters and Ginger in years past.

"How about these wreaths?" She held them both aloft.

"We'll put the one with shells and sea glass on the front door," Ginger suggested. "If anyone wants the other one, it's yours. Otherwise, let's start a box for giveaways."

"I call dibs on it," Kai said, shooting up her hand.

"Sold to the highest bidder." Marina handed it to Kai, then held up a vintage tin decoration. "And this silver bell?"

Ginger shrugged. "Let it go to a good home."

"I'd love that," Heather said, clasping her hands.

"Then it's yours, dear." Ginger hugged her. "I'll miss you when you move next year. Are you sure you wouldn't want to stay? You and Blake could save some money for your first house."

"Actually, I have a big surprise." Excitement flashed across Heather's face as she glanced at her mother. "We were going to tell you together, but I can't wait. Blake told me his parents have promised a very generous down payment as a wedding gift. They said we can start looking for a house before the wedding."

"Why, that's wonderful." For a moment, Marina wished she could have done that. Yet, it was all she could do to put the twins through school after their father failed to return from the war in Afghanistan. She'd also spent money to open the cafe and was employing Heather now.

Marina caught herself. The wedding wasn't about her or Blake's parents.

Swallowing her pride, she said, "Please tell them how much I appreciate their generosity. It means a lot to me to see you in your own home."

"Thank you, Mom. I know they'll appreciate that."

"That's very thoughtful of them." Ginger put her arm around Marina's shoulder.

She leaned into the familiar warmth of her grandmother's embrace. Since they'd both lost spouses, Ginger understood how she felt. She had been there to help with the twins; she was Marina's rock.

They all loved Ginger, each in their own way. Their grandmother had stepped in to raise Kai and see Brooke through high school and her marriage.

Ginger's home was their home, too. They all agreed that the holidays were sweeter here at the Coral Cottage with Ginger.

However, that might change soon. Recently, Ginger confided in Marina that Oliver's nephew was concerned about him living alone as he grew older. Oliver and his late wife didn't have children, so Chris wanted him to move close to his family in Boston. Would Oliver consider that? Marina wondered.

If so, what would Ginger do?

Marina smoothed her hand over Ginger's. She hadn't told her sisters about this possibility because she didn't want them to worry during the holidays.

"Marina, what do you think?" Kai asked.

She shook her head. "Sorry, what?"

"Pink or purple highlights—yes or no? I won't be on stage for a while, so I thought I'd have some fun."

"Why not both?" Marina loved Kai's wavy blond hair, but Kai had her own style. "Temporary or permanent?"

"Good idea. I'll ask Brandy." Kai's gaze roved over Marina's hair. "Why don't you come with me to Beach Waves?"

"Does it look like I need to?" She ran a hand over her shoulder-length reddish brown hair. Her highlights were long gone.

"Couldn't hurt." Kai's cheeks colored with embarrassment. "What I meant was, with the holidays here and all the parties at the cafe, you'll want to look your best."

Kai was probably right. "That's a good idea. I'll come with you. Anyone else? We can have a party at Beach Waves."

Brooke tossed her long braid over her shoulder. "Low maintenance suits me. I don't need to dress up to work in the garden."

"I'll join you," Ginger said, smiling. "My treat for anyone who wants to go."

Kai's eyes lit with appreciation. "I love having a plan to get out of the house. I'll make reservations for us."

Marina suspected Kai needed emotional support and occasional relief from her new motherhood role. "Do you think we can get in so close to Christmas?"

"I've already checked, and Brandy is working through the holidays," Kai replied. "I don't think she has family nearby. I know she used to live in Los Angeles, so maybe she drives up for the day to see friends."

"I know what it's like spending the holidays without much family around," Marina said. Ginger always came to visit her and the twins in San Francisco, but other than Ginger, they had been alone.

"We were fine, Mom," Heather said, pulling out a strand of garland with faux berries. "We had our friends. But now I know how much fun it is in Summer Beach. I'm glad you got fired."

"I *quit* my anchor position," Marina said. "By a split second, but still, that counts. And I'm so happy I did."

"We all are," Brooke said as Heather and Kai nodded.

Marina smiled at her family. "Let's make this a merry Christmas, even though Ethan likely won't make it home."

The front door flew open, and Blake stood in the entryway, his arms filled with more boxes. "Where would you like these?"

"Right here," Heather said, kissing him. "Thanks, Babe. What do you want to do with these, Ginger?"

"Put them there and start unpacking." Ginger glanced around the room with fondness. "Have fun and surprise me. I should check on the crew outside."

Their grandmother usually had exacting instructions. Before Marina could ask another question, laughter erupted outside, and the kitchen timer buzzed.

"That's the cranberry bread," she said, hurrying to the kitchen.

While tending to her baked goods, Christmas lights drew Marina's attention. The sun had set, and the colorful lights glowed on the lawn. She opened the rear door and stepped outside, shivering slightly.

Christmas lights cascaded from the roof line, lined the windows, and illuminated the old surfboards they'd once decorated. The men had used their creativity to arrange the decorations in a new manner, but it was just as pretty and fun.

Jack put his arm around her. "What do you think?"

"It's magical. This year is special."

Ginger turned to her. "Every year is special, dear. Every year, every day, every moment of our lives. Savor them all."

Marina clasped her grandmother's hand. "This is one of those wonderful moments."

"There's always more to come," Ginger added with a mysterious smile. "Are you ready for it?"

2

"*H*ello, Coral Cafe." Marina tucked the phone between her shoulder and jaw as she plated the last butternut squash salad of the lunch run. "How may we help you? Uh-oh…" The phone slipped from her tenuous grip.

As she fumbled the device, Cruise whipped around from the stove. "Got it," he said, catching her phone in mid-air. Grinning, he held the phone to her ear.

It was her friend Ivy at the Seabreeze Inn. She laughed and said, "Marina, your grandmother's painting is ready. I've left messages, but she hasn't called, so I'm a little worried. Is she okay?"

"Ginger is fine, but she seldom checks her voicemail." Cradling the phone, Marina finished the winter vegetable salad with a flourish of pumpkin seeds. With Cruise handling the kitchen and a part-time server on tables, she could leave the cafe after lunch. "I could pick it up this afternoon for her. I'll check with Ginger."

"Perfect," Ivy replied.

After hanging up, Marina turned to Cruise. "Would you handle everything from here?"

"Yes, Chef," he replied automatically.

"And Cruise?" Marina grinned at him. "Nice catch."

He juggled his tongs. "Anytime."

She changed out of her chef jacket and into a pink hoodie embroidered with the town's logo and tagline: *Life is Better in Summer Beach.*

After confirming with Ginger and swapping her Mini-Cooper for Jack's vintage VW van, she and Ginger started for the Seabreeze Inn.

Her grandmother settled in the seat beside her, dressed in pressed denims and kitten-heel boots with a smart ivory wool jacket. "I loved the creativity you all brought to our decorating party. I'm enjoying the fresh perspective."

"This holiday season feels different," Marina said as she drove along the sunny coastline and turned onto Main Street.

She loved spending the holidays at the beach. The summer crowds had thinned, and the village looked magical. Glittery Christmas, Hanukkah, and Kwanzaa decorations sparkled in every storefront. They passed Brandy's hair salon, which looked busy.

"Kai called this morning," Ginger said. "She made our appointments for an afternoon of pampering at Beach Waves."

"Sounds good." She glanced at her grandmother, whose ginger-colored hair was always styled. "Is it just me, or does something feel off this year?"

"Are you worried because I'm cleaning house? I saw the way you looked at the donations yesterday. I'm fine, dear. Nothing to worry about."

Marina let out a breath. "Thanks for clearing that up."

"Your expressions are easy to read," Ginger said pointedly. "Don't ever bet on cards."

"I only bet on my business. That's risky enough."

Ginger swayed to "White Christmas," the Bing Crosby version Marina had put on for her. "Every year brings changes, dear. We'll have babies around the tree for the first time in years. And Heather is building quite a business with the cafe's food trucks. Her holiday coffee and treats menu was a brilliant idea. You raised a smart young woman."

"I'm proud of her. Ethan, too." Recalling their last phone conversation, Marina sighed. Her son had always loved golf and recently fulfilled his dream of turning professional. "Sadly, he's unable to come home for Christmas."

"Is that what's troubling you?" Ginger touched her shoulder. "Ethan is having the time of his life. Is it a new girlfriend?"

"With his demanding travel and practice schedule, he says he doesn't have time." Even so, Marina was happy for him. "This will be the first Christmas the twins haven't spent together. Maybe that's why it feels off."

Ginger nodded thoughtfully. "I remember when you moved to San Francisco. We adjusted, and you will, too. Growing pains aren't only for children. It's normal as we move through life's phases. The key is to expect and embrace change, not fight against it."

Marina inclined her head. "For years, you celebrated Christmas Eve with Brooke and her children, and then flew to visit us on Christmas Day. In hindsight, I realize that was a burden on you. I shouldn't have asked you to do that."

"You didn't. It was what I wanted to do." Ginger's eyes sparkled at the memories. "Traveling on Christmas Day is a joy. Most people are full of good cheer, except those who seldom are anyway. I try to find something to enjoy every day because there is plenty to complain about. Yet, all that does is give you ulcers and premature wrinkles." She paused. "What do you enjoy every day?"

"Jack and Leo, of course. Working with Heather and following Ethan's career. Being here with you and my sisters and their families." Marina glanced from the window toward the sea. "And I love waking to the sound of the ocean."

Ginger nodded. "This is our mild, sunny winter. Why, I remember fresh snowy days in Paris. They were gorgeous and wildly romantic but also came with wet boots and chapped cheeks. One could choose to love it or complain incessantly."

Marina smiled at Ginger's eternally upbeat approach to life. Today hardly felt like winter to anyone but the locals. She loved this time of year. Fewer people were on the beach, lemons were turning yellow, and poinsettias fluttered in the breeze.

"This year, we'll have new faces gathered around our traditional feast," Ginger said.

"Two new babies and one young-at-heart boyfriend—I mean, your *beau*." Marina corrected herself with the word her grandmother preferred.

Ginger rested a hand on Marina's shoulder. "Oliver is more than a beau now."

"Is there something you want to share?" Marina asked.

"Soon, perhaps." Her grandmother shrugged with a small smile.

Even at Ginger's age, she was vibrant and attractive, ageless in spirit and mind. She could still out-trek Marina up the cliff to her favorite meditation spot overlooking the Pacific Ocean.

From time to time, Ginger also flew to the East Coast to train young code breakers working on government projects. Only recently, during his research for his biography of Ginger, Jack learned that she had been studying potential applications of artificial intelligence for years.

Her grandmother patted her arm, and Marina tried to shake off the odd sensation she felt. Still, even Jack had noticed it this morning. He'd joked with her, calling it a premonition.

Maybe it was.

She lifted her chin and shook her hair back. Christmas was a time for secrets and surprises, that's all.

"Thank you for helping me pick up the painting today," Ginger said, cutting the small silence between them. "Oliver adores Ivy's seascapes. I'm sure he doesn't expect this."

"It's been a well-guarded secret," Marina assured her. "Others, not so much. Last night, Scout dragged out the colorful case we bought for Leo's surprise laptop."

"Didn't you and Jack hide it?"

"Sure, but that dog opens doors, and we don't have many hiding places in the cottage. Still, Leo was ecstatic over his early gift. He loves his new computer."

Ginger laughed. "Unexpected mishaps are half the fun of holidays. As long as no one is hurt."

"I had plenty with the twins when they were young." *Life moved fast,* she thought.

Jack's son was nearly a teenager. Heather had graduated from university and became engaged last year. Although she and Blake had initially planned a summer wedding, with her managing the Coral Cafe food trucks and Blake overseeing a new marina life rescue and research organization, they'd decided to put off the wedding until spring.

Marina eased the van in front of the Seabreeze Inn, and a woman on a ladder turned to wave at them. Shelly secured one end of a green garland over the front door before climbing down to greet them. Velvet-red poinsettias lined the path to the entry and spilled from the veranda. Beribboned wreaths hung from every window.

"Shelly has outdone herself on decorations this year," Ginger said. "I'm sure Amelia Erickson is pleased with her efforts."

Marina smiled at the mention of the former property owner. "You speak as if she's still with us."

"Maybe she is." Ginger unbuckled her seatbelt. "She was such a force; I'm not surprised that her presence is still sensed here. That's what Shelly tells me. Fortunately, Amelia's spirit seems benevolent."

"I wouldn't mention that to Ivy." Marina grinned as she turned off the engine.

Although Ivy, her sister, and niece had transformed the grand old home into a popular inn, a roaming spirit was a sensitive subject between them. Ivy worried a haunted inn would be bad for business; Shelly argued the opposite. They'd disagreed about that since Marina arrived in town.

When they started toward the entryway, Shelly moved the ladder to one side, greeted them with hugs, and opened the door. "Ivy told me you're picking up the painting for Oliver."

"I hope my suggestion worked out," Ginger said, her eyes brightening.

Shelly smiled. "I think it's one of her best." She excused herself to continue her work outside.

Ivy was in the foyer with their niece Poppy, who ran the marketing efforts for the inn. The room was festooned with lavish garlands and brightened with poinsettias. A hint of cinnamon and nutmeg filled the air.

"What lovely decorations," Ginger exclaimed.

Ivy greeted them and they chatted a little about the upcoming open house, a popular affair that Marina, Ginger, and the rest of the family would attend.

After chatting a little, Ivy said, "I'll bring the painting out for you. Would you like to come with me or wait in the parlor?" She motioned toward an adjoining room tastefully decorated with antiques and seascapes.

"We'll wait," Ginger said, sitting on the sofa. "We can visit with Poppy."

But before Poppy could join them, the front door opened, and a slender young woman with a pixie haircut, black turtleneck, and paint splattered jeans stepped inside. She gazed around the grand entry with a tentative expression.

Poppy stepped from the reception desk. "Welcome to the Seabreeze Inn. Do you have a reservation?"

"No, but I hope you have a room for a few days." She rested her backpack by the door. "I was on my way to an arts and crafts show in Los Angeles, but my vehicle had other ideas. The mechanic says it will take several days to find the right parts and repair it." The young woman's dark blue eyes scanned the entryway with keen interest.

"I'm sorry, we're fully booked," Poppy replied. "You could try the Seal Cove Inn."

"They sent me here." The woman lifted her eyebrows.

"I've never been to Summer Beach. Could you recommend another inn here?"

Ginger brushed her hand against Marina's. She glanced at her grandmother, whose eyes held a curious look of interest.

"Are you an artist?" Ginger asked the younger woman.

Mildly surprised, she nodded. "My hand painted Christmas ornaments and snow globes are popular this time of year." A smile wreathed her delicate facial features. "I'm Holly Berry—my parents had a sense of humor."

Marina couldn't resist asking, "Were you a Christmas baby?"

"That's what my birth certificate says," Holly said, shifting.

"What a shame you're stranded here for the holidays," Ginger said. "Where is your family home?"

"Phoenix, but I don't have any family. I usually spend holidays with a couple of friends I met in foster care. They're the closest thing to family I have. I was moved around a lot." Holly bit her lip and shrugged. "But with my misbehaving car, that won't be happening this year."

Her grandmother swiftly extended her hand. "I'm Ginger Delavie, and I have a room for you at the Coral Cottage."

Marina wondered if that was wise. They knew nothing about the younger woman besides what she said.

But then, Marina thought about her father's history. Dennis Moore had been raised in foster care, too. He'd worked hard to put himself through the university to become a certified public accountant. She couldn't judge Holly for that. Whatever had happened to the girl's parents wasn't important. Still, something struck her as vaguely familiar about the young woman.

"Is your inn very far?" Holly asked. "I walked here, of course."

"It's fairly close, and we're happy to give you a lift," Ginger replied, avoiding Marina's look of surprise.

Finally, Marina had to speak up, "It's not really—"

"And my granddaughter Marina runs the adjoining cafe," Ginger said, gesturing to her with a look that said, *This is my decision.*

"Well, it's nice to meet you, Holly," Marina said, giving in to her grandmother's will.

Just then, Ivy returned with the painting. "Here you are, just as you wanted. Summer Beach, as seen from the driver's seat of Oliver's car. And that woman in the distance is you."

They all turned toward the painting, a likeness of Summer Beach, with Ginger's cottage on one side and a vintage Jaguar convertible on the other. Two forms strolled the beach—Ginger and...

"Is that Oliver?" Marina had been so accustomed to seeing Ginger with Bertrand in photographs and portraits, that it took her by surprise, even though it shouldn't.

Ginger raised her brow and smiled. "Of course."

Marina's grandfather had passed away years ago, and Ginger had the right to date. Or choose another...what? Significant other? Husband?

Her grandmother was still scrutinizing her. "Does that surprise you?"

Marina's cheeks warmed with embarrassment. "No, but he's sure to be surprised. In a good way, for sure."

Ever gracious, Ginger pressed her lips together in a

knowing way and lifted her chin. "With this, he'll remember Summer Beach wherever he goes."

Admiring the work of art, she wondered about Ginger's motivation for this. "Is Oliver moving?" Ivy asked.

"The lease on his beach bungalow will be up soon. He will have to make a decision."

Now everything was making sense. She recalled Oliver's upcoming trip to Boston to visit his nephew's family—the son of his late brother Kurt.

Is that what this painting was about? She couldn't imagine Oliver moving and letting Ginger go, but family was important at their age.

A chill crept over her. Would Ginger move with him? She was so shaken by this thought she couldn't even ask the question. She hadn't thought this decision would come this soon.

Marina and her sisters needed Ginger, too.

Turning back to Ivy, Ginger put a hand to her heart and nodded her approval. "You've amazed me again with your talent. I'm sure he'll love it."

While Ivy wrapped the piece with care, Marina found her voice again. "We brought Jack's van to transport it." She reached for the painting, eager to do something to alleviate the tension she felt.

Ginger turned to Holly. "We have room for you, too. Come along; we're going there now."

The younger woman dipped her chin. "I appreciate that, but I have to ask your rates."

Placing a hand on Holly's shoulder, Ginger said, "You'll be staying in my home. I have plenty of room now that my girls have moved on. Our Heather is about your age and has a room down the hall. Think of us as family while you're here."

Once again, Marina was surprised, but Holly's face filled with relief and joy. "Oh, thank you. I'm so happy to have met you."

Looking jolly, Ginger hooked her arm through Holly's. "It's such a nuisance having your car break down just before the holidays. But now we can learn all about each other. Won't that be fun?"

As Ginger and Holly led the way, Marina exchanged a look with Ivy and shrugged. Ginger did things her way.

Holly seemed a little lost, though she was certainly artistic and adventurous, setting off on her own to sell her wares at arts and crafts markets. She wasn't likely a serial killer, so where was the harm in inviting a stranger home? Ginger was generally a good judge of character, and she did as she pleased.

Then another thought struck her. Wouldn't Marina want someone to look after her daughter like that?

"Just a moment. At the door, Holly stopped and dug into her large backpack. "I know it's here somewhere." As Ginger waited, she opened one small box, then another.

"What delightful ornaments," Ginger said, peering at one with interest. "Are these the ones you make?"

Holly nodded. "I often paint images of people and places I recall."

"Here, this one is meant for you, I think." She handed Ivy an ornament with a hand painted scene, suspended from a golden ribbon.

"What a lovely beach house by the sea…" Ivy paused, lifting a pair of red reading glasses for a closer look.

Surprise flashed across her face. "Why, you've painted the inn."

Holly shrugged with a small smile. "Sort of looks like it."

Ivy peered closer. "No, it's identical. This is astonishing. How did you do this?"

"I paint from memory," Holly replied, her cheeks flushing pink.

That comment didn't sit well with Marina's journalistic training. "I thought you said you've never been to Summer Beach." She noticed Ginger's mild admonishment from the corner of her eye but couldn't help herself. Her grandmother had just invited this stranger—who was clearly caught in a lie—into her home.

Was Ginger losing her judgment and perspective?

Poppy leaned forward. "You probably saw our photos on the internet or social media. I post everywhere."

Relief washed over Holly's face. "I have a photographic memory for images."

"As an artist, I can appreciate that," Ivy said, turning over the ornament. "It's quite good. We'll hang this on our tree with pleasure. Thank you."

Marina lifted the painting into the van with Holly's help. On the way to her grandmother's home, Marina listened as Ginger chatted and asked questions. Holly peered out the windows with apparent interest.

When there was a lull in the conversation, Marina asked, "So, you live in Phoenix?"

"Sometimes," Holly replied. "I travel to shows a lot."

"I love visiting there. What part of Phoenix?"

"Oh, different parts. I stay with friends."

Marina considered that vague—evasive even. "And you don't know the area?"

"Not really. I'm either painting or going to shows."

Overall, Holly was pleasant enough, Marina figured, although she offered few details about her life. That was disconcerting.

And then, Marina remembered her father again, and guilt nibbled at her mind. She knew it could be challenging for kids aging out of foster care to find their place in the world.

When they arrived home, Ginger nodded toward the cottage and glanced at Holly. "Does this look familiar?" she asked lightly.

Holly stared at the Coral Cottage, her lips slowly parting. Recognition flashed across her face.

While Marina watched, Ginger held out her hand. "Let's see the other ornament you took from your bag."

Marina had seen Ginger glance at that one earlier when Holly was searching for the one she gave Ivy.

The younger woman dug into her backpack again and withdrew the first piece. She stared at it for a moment before showing it to Ginger.

"What a remarkable likeness and excellent detail," Ginger said, comparing the ornament to her home. "Just look at this, Marina. Isn't it lovely?"

Marina narrowed her eyes. Holly had likely seen the Coral Cafe online, although this miniature scene was of the front of Ginger's home rather than the cafe. There were two figures beside it—a woman and a man. Still, anyone could have taken a photo and posted it. She'd seen tourists set up shots of Ginger's coral-painted cottage against the blue sea and sky. The juxtaposition of colors created striking photos.

Ginger held up the ornament. "This could be me and Oliver. How funny. It seems you painted Summer Beach before you arrived."

"I had no idea," Holly said, her face paling. "But you should have that. As a gift. For good luck."

"Maybe this is why your car stalled here," Ginger said thoughtfully.

"Likely, it's another coincidence," Marina said. She got out to carry Oliver's painting to a hiding place in the cottage.

Ginger believed people were right where they were supposed to be. However, Marina questioned this. Accidents happened and cars broke down.

"I just paint from memory," Holly said again, almost to herself.

Ginger tapped her chin in thought. "Some call what you have *second sight.*"

Holly turned away, but Marina could see the tips of her ears turning pink. For some reason, Ginger's comments disturbed her.

Deeply.

As if I don't have enough to do this holiday season, Marina thought. Suddenly, another possibility came to mind.

Maybe Holly was the reason she'd been feeling out of sorts today. Had Jack been right about a premonition? If she'd really sensed Holly's arrival, now she felt even more off kilter.

And just when things were going so well this holiday season.

a swift wind kicked up the waves, misting Jack's hair. He flipped up the collar on his windbreaker to shield his neck. The sun painted long shadows across the sand, and the salt air was just cool enough to remind him that Christmas was coming.

Someone called out to him. "Hey, Jack, wait up."

Jack looked up toward a dune. Oliver had just cleared it and was walking toward him. He motioned for Oliver to join him.

"Want some company?" Oliver asked. "I try to get in my daily step count, but I didn't walk the course today. I played with a buddy who has a golf cart."

"No worries, it's always good to see you. I'm out here with Leo and Scout."

Still wearing his golf clothes, Oliver fell into step beside him.

Despite the age difference, the two men had become close friends. They watched Leo toss sticks down the beach, sending Scout bounding after them with his uneven gait.

The yellow Lab's enthusiasm never failed to make Jack smile.

"Good throw, buddy!" Jack called out as Leo jogged ahead.

Another few years, and the lanky kid would be his height. Maybe even taller. Now that Leo was in his life, Jack was acutely aware of the passage of time. His son's milestones marked it for him.

Oliver chuckled as he watched Leo play with Scout. "Your son is growing into a fine young man. You seem to be on good terms with his mother. I admire that."

"We were always friends and work colleagues, except for one stressful night. We were reporting on a tense, dangerous situation." Jack shoved his hands into his pockets, thinking about what seemed a lifetime ago. "We weren't sure we'd see the morning light."

"And you didn't know about him until a few years ago?"

"It was a shock, but we got past that," Jack replied. "Vanessa is a great mother, and we're comfortable co-parenting now. Leo is one of the best things to ever happen to me, along with Marina."

"You're still a man in his prime—do you miss the thrill of reporting from the front lines?"

Jack chuckled as he drew a hand through his damp hair. "I don't miss ducking whizzing bullets. Once, I lived for that, but I'd be a fool to leave my life here. I'm finally doing what I always dreamed of—researching and writing books."

"Congratulations on the successful book launch, by the way," Oliver said. "How is it doing on the charts?"

"I'll know in a few days." He'd just returned from New York, where he'd made the rounds of morning shows, magazines, and radio talk shows to discuss the biography he'd written with Ginger, *Decoding a Remarkable Life.* The publisher risked a large print run on him, so he had to support the effort.

Oliver grinned. "Have you heard who might play Ginger in the film?"

"If they could bring Maureen O'Hara back, she'd be perfect."

Oliver's face lit. "I always thought Ginger favored her—more in grit and determination than actual appearance—though their hair was similar. In fact, we just saw Maureen O'Hara in *Miracle on 34th Street,* one of my favorite holiday films." Oliver paused, and a smile lifted his lips. "Ginger will always be a beautiful woman. I'm a lucky man."

"You two are a good match," Jack said, and he meant it. "I can't imagine Ginger putting up with anyone else."

"Hey, Dad," Leo yelled. "Watch this." He tossed three pieces of driftwood in different directions, and Scout took off, making the rounds like he was touching bases—and loving every minute of it.

"Look at him go," Jack yelled back, pumping a fist.

They watched Leo and Scout for a few minutes before resuming their walk toward the marina.

"I have to confess," Jack began, changing the subject. "I'm having trouble finding the perfect gift for Marina. I know what would make my wife the happiest—seeing Ethan for Christmas, but he's busy. Any suggestions?"

Oliver nodded knowingly, watching a pelican dive into the waves. "He's got real potential on the pro circuit. In sports, a man must make his mark when young."

"That's true." He and Marina had traveled to tournaments with Ginger and Oliver to watch Ethan play. Oliver's golf expertise helped them appreciate just how good Ethan had become. And Oliver was always willing to hit golf balls with him.

"Have you and Ginger discussed any special plans this holiday?" Jack asked.

Oliver stroked his chin in thought. "I had an idea, but with your book out, I want to give her the time to make appearances if she needs to. Book signings, I suppose."

Jack shook his head. "She doesn't want to do any promotion, aside from talks she might want to give to students. She told me living her life is her job; writing about it was mine."

Oliver chuckled. "That's Ginger. She's more interested in the next idea or experience."

"I sympathize with you. What can you possibly give a woman like that?"

"I'll figure it out," Oliver replied. "This isn't my first rodeo, Jack."

"I suppose not. The Delavie-Moore women are gems, each in their own way." Jack remembered the first time he'd seen Marina hobbling from her room at the Seabreeze Inn after she'd lost her job in San Francisco and sprained her ankle. His world had shifted on its axis.

The best gifts life had to offer couldn't be wrapped.

As they approached the marina, Scout's bark announced their arrival. They spotted Axe talking with another man near a boat.

Axe had built the Shell Amphitheater that he and Kai ran. Last summer, they produced the musical *Mary Poppins* they'd planned before Stella was born. Marina confided that, with the new baby, the production had been more difficult than Kai thought it would be. That was behind her decision to take the holidays off.

Jack couldn't blame her. Leo taught him how much commitment children require.

This year, Axe leased out the venue to friends producing a Christmas choral extravaganza. He and Kai planned to produce another holiday musical next year when Stella was a little older.

"Hey there," Jack called to Axe and his friend Tyler, who'd made his fortune in tech.

Tyler waved them over. "Axe and I are discussing some plans. I want to renovate the house and add a wing."

"I can certainly help you with that, but my crew is booked for a couple of weeks after the holidays," Axe said. "You'll have to wait your turn."

Tyler grinned. "You know I don't like to do that."

"This time, it's nonnegotiable," Axe said. "I have a surprise project for Kai after the holidays. Don't breathe a word about this. I'm building her a studio on the back of our property for her recording and dance choreography. Besides, your project will take much longer. We'll need architectural plans and approvals before we do anything."

"Put me in line, then," Tyler said with a fist bump.

"You got it. In the meantime, let's discuss what you want." Axe turned to Jack and Oliver. "What are you guys up to?"

Oliver crossed his arms. "Aside from solving world problems, we're trying to decide what to give the special women in our lives."

Jack dragged his knuckles across his stubbled chin. "Maybe some sort of kitchen gadget, a sweater, new shoes…"

Oliver chuckled at his list.

"What's wrong with that? Marina told me she needs new shoes for work. Some sort of heavy-duty clogs."

"Oh, no, my man," Tyler said. "That's like buying a woman a toaster. I made that mistake once when we were young and poor. Don't go there. You could take her shopping, but that has no romance, no originality."

"Worse," Oliver chimed in. "She would think you forgot about her. No, they deserve something memorable. Romantic, but not in a way she would expect. Something to make her laugh and throw her arms around you."

Jack scrubbed his face in exasperation. "You've had more experience than all of us."

"Doesn't mean I have good ideas for Marina," Oliver said. "And you know what Ginger is like. She's seen the world."

Axe snapped his fingers. "Say, I have an idea. We're all in Summer Beach for Christmas, right?"

They all nodded, and Jack wondered what his brother-in-law had in mind.

"How much is this going to cost me?" Tyler asked.

"Don't worry, you can afford it, old man," Jack replied, giving him a playful punch in the arm.

"Hey, who's old?" Tyler tugged a few gray hairs on Jack's head while he swatted him away.

"Come on, guys, listen to this." With a mischievous expression, Axe shared his idea. "This might be out of your comfort zones, but I guarantee it's something they'll never expect—and never forget."

Oliver's eyes lit up. "We should get Chip involved, too. Make this a surprise for all our sweethearts."

"What do we need to do?" Jack asked, intrigued.

Axe waved his hands in a conspiratorial gesture. "First,

we get everyone together. Heather's fiancé, too. Trust me on this one."

Just then, Leo and Scout bounded across the beach. "Hey, Dad, can we get ice cream now?"

"Soon, little man." Jack shivered. "Make it hot chocolate with a dollop of ice cream, and you've got a deal. Marina makes the best. We'll go to the cafe soon."

Leo grinned. "Cool!"

"The kid is in, too," Axe said, pulling Leo into the group.

Oliver put his arm around the boy, who looked slightly confused. "I have a feeling we're about to get ourselves into something interesting, son."

Jack laughed and tousled Leo's hair. "Don't we always have a good time?"

4

*M*arina arranged her thinly sliced, toasted cranberry bread squares on a serving board with an array of cheeses. She joined her sister at the communal chef's table in the kitchen, open to the cafe. "Here's a snack before the dinner crowd arrives. And some avocado for Stella."

Kai bounced the baby on her lap. "Thanks. We're famished."

She tucked Stella into a baby carrier beside her, taking care to keep her out of the way of servers who might be whisking in and out with plates of food. Stella squealed with glee at the avocado slices.

After taking a bite of cheese, Kai asked, "Where are all the guys?"

"Jack usually walks Scout about this time, and Leo is probably with him," Marina replied.

"I've been trying to reach Axe," Kai said. "And Ginger asked me if I'd seen Oliver after his golf game."

"Maybe they're all plotting together."

Kai made a face. "Those guys? Please, they're the last ones I'd suspect of anything."

Marina arched an eyebrow at that. "Uh-oh. Bored much?"

She'd been concerned about her sister. As much as Kai had longed for a baby, Marina suspected she might be overwhelmed with the duties of motherhood. Or worse, she would miss the excitement of traveling and performing on the musical theater circuit.

Kai shrugged. "Sometimes I wish something would happen around here. I love Summer Beach, but it's hardly Broadway."

"Nothing is," Marina said, peering at her sister. "Are you feeling blue because you took the holidays off?"

"I had to. That English nanny almost killed me, but now, I miss it."

"You were fabulous in *Mary Poppins*, but maybe it was too soon for you to take it on. With Stella getting older, it will be easier."

Kai's face bloomed at the memory. "It was a fun production, even with all the kid herding. Little scene stealers, every one of them." Kai made a face.

"Even Leo?"

"Oh, my gosh, especially Leo." Kai's eyes widened. "When I cast him as Tiny Tim last year, I created a monster."

Marina laughed, knowing Kai didn't mean a word of what she said.

With a theatrical sigh, her sister rested her chin on the heel of her hand. "I love Stella, but I underestimated this entire mommy gig. If it hadn't been for Brooke and Ginger, I don't know what I would've done. By next year, Stella should be walking and talking. When do they start speaking again?"

"Give her a little longer to piece together sentences." Marina grinned, recalling how she managed with twins. Those early years weren't easy, but she remembered them fondly now.

Marina spread homemade ricotta onto a small cranberry toast, drizzled honey, and sprinkled flaked sea salt. "Here, try this."

"Do you have any wine to go with it?" Kai asked. When Marina looked surprised, she added, "What? Like you never did that? Besides, I'm on holiday."

She realized her sister needed an artistic outlet, or at the least, a little break from the daily duties of motherhood—much as she loved her daughter. "How about my bubbly holiday special?"

"Absolutely." Kai snapped her fingers, swaying to the Christmas pop songs on the sound system. "I'm feeling better already." Smiling now, she wiped Stella's green, avocado-smeared face and hands and kissed her cheek. "What a happy mess you are." She put a few banana slices on the carrier tray in front of her, and Stella broke into a toothless grin.

"I know of a good babysitter you might like. A retired nurse. She might have time during the holiday season."

"Really?" Kai brightened. "I'd love her number."

"I'll give it to you." Marina brought a bottle of chilled cava—the Spanish version of champagne—to the counter and poured a small glass for Kai. She added a splash of deep red Chambord and a sprig of mint. "A Kir Royale for a royal pain in the—"

Interrupting, Kai said breezily, "Thanks, Sis. You're the best. You're not joining me?"

"Not while I have to cook. That's how accidents happen in the kitchen. So, do you want to hear some news?"

"Please, I'm dying here. I've already outlined the next two years of productions, and I'm choreographing dances and blocking scenes in the living room. I've broken a vase and a candy dish with my high kicks. At this rate, Stella will be an assistant director by the time she starts kindergarten."

Marina jerked her head toward their grandmother's cottage. "Ginger has a visitor."

Kai choked on her cocktail. "Not another man?"

"What? No!" Marina chuckled at the absurdity of that. "Holly is her name." Quickly, Marina told her about their meeting and how Ginger had invited her to stay.

"I think that's kind," Kai said. "I probably would have done the same thing. Wouldn't you?"

Marina shook her head. "Now I feel guilty that I didn't."

"That surprises me. You're usually a good judge of people. This Holly—she's okay, right?"

"I think so. She's an artist, and she was on her way to a holiday market in Los Angeles."

"Why doesn't she just stay here and set up a booth at ours?"

"Well, I suppose she could. But Kai, there's something odd about her."

"Like what?"

"She paints ornaments with images."

"You mean, like wreaths and trees? Yeah, that's weird."

Marina leaned forward and lowered her voice. "No,

silly. Houses. The Seabreeze Inn—and even Ginger's house."

"So? Artists paint what they see. She's obviously been here before."

"No, she insists she hasn't been. But then she says she paints from memory."

Kai held her glass in midair. Even Stella looked up with rounded eyes. "Okay, that is weird. What's up with that?"

"I don't know. That's why I think we should watch her. She's not telling the truth, but I don't know why she would lie. Why not just say you painted it from something you saw online? Or admit you've been here before. We don't know her; we're not judging her."

"Really?" Kai raised her eyebrows.

"Okay, maybe a little."

"Does she seem threatening or anything?"

Marina wiped Stella's sweet little face again. "No, just… lost," she added, looking for the right word. "Artistic, of course. Kind, I think."

Holly had given Ivy and Ginger the ornaments, almost as if she'd been expecting to.

Kai scooped more cheese from the board. "I'll invite her to the market in the morning."

Marina touched a finger to her lips. "You can do that right now. Here they come."

"Doesn't this look cozy," Ginger exclaimed when they arrived. "I wanted to show Holly your cafe before I began dinner."

"I can bring dinner to you, or you can join us here," Marina said. "Holly, too, of course." If Ginger didn't eat at the cafe or go out with Oliver or friends, Marina often brought dinner to her.

Marina gestured to seats at the table. "Would you like to join us at the chef's table? It's where family and friends sit."

"It's a little chilly this evening," Holly said with a shiver.

"We turn on the heat lamps," Marina said. "It's quite cozy on the patio this time of year. And we have wraps if you need one. A local woman makes them for us."

Cruise walked in through the rear door for his shift. "I'll get them for you," he offered. A few moments later, he reappeared with beautifully woven shawls.

"Thank you, dear," Ginger said, putting one around her shoulders. Holly did the same, admiring it as she did.

After they sat down, Kai said, "Our friend has a booth to sell these shawls at the holiday market. I'd like to buy a couple for gifts."

Ginger turned to Holly. "Since you have to forgo your market in Los Angeles, perhaps you can sell your ornaments here." To Kai, she added, "They're quite lovely."

"So I've heard," Kai said.

Marina nudged her under the table. "That's a great idea, and Kai will be happy to help."

"I can't tell you how much I appreciate this," Holly said with relief. "Everyone in Summer Beach has made me feel so welcome, and just when I didn't know where to turn."

Feeling a little guilty, Marina glanced at Kai before continuing. "Our sister Brooke delivers her fresh produce and picks up my baked goods early in the morning from the cafe. She can give you a lift to the market."

"Most of my inventory is in my vehicle," Holly said. "I would have to get it from the garage."

"We'll figure it out," Kai said, soothing her concern.

Marina nodded in agreement. Giving residents a

chance to earn money from their arts and crafts was the impetus behind the holiday market.

This season, Holly was one of them.

"Hi everyone," Heather said, breezing into the kitchen. "We have a party to cater tonight, but I wanted to welcome Holly. Ginger told me you're staying upstairs with us. I'll be back late, so I hope I don't wake you."

"When I'm in dreamland, nothing wakes me," Holly said, smiling shyly.

The two younger women chatted while people began arriving for dinner. Marina excused herself to put on her chef jacket.

While she was changing, Kai slipped into the room.

"Well, what do you think?" Marina asked.

"Holly seems sweet," Kai said. "Maybe she misspoke earlier. You and Ginger are a formidable pair."

"But her story about never having been here, yet painting from memory, doesn't make sense. Still, I want to help her because she seems adrift."

Kai waved off her concerns. "People don't always say exactly what they mean. I'm sure we'll have a good day at the market."

Marina wondered. She would hear all about it, for sure. They returned to the front with the others. She saw Jack and the other men heading toward them.

"Hey, look who's here." Kai scooped Stella from her carrier and wiped banana from her smiling, happy face. "It's Daddy."

"With Leo and Oliver," Marina added. "I'll bet they're hungry."

Her special this evening was roasted turkey over wild rice and a side of rosemary-infused red potatoes. With that was a garden salad with pomegranate seeds and mandarin orange slices.

"Here's the light of my life," Jack said, kissing Marina's cheek.

"Now I know you're hungry." She laughed, hugging him and Leo.

Oliver greeted Ginger with a kiss, and Axe did the same with Kai before taking Stella to lift her into the air. The baby squealed with glee.

"She's as expressive as her mother," Axe said, laughing and cooing at his daughter.

"What have you guys been up to?" Kai asked.

"We ran into each other on the beach," Axe replied. "I met Tyler to discuss a new project and saw these guys walking."

"That's good exercise for you," Ginger said, giving Oliver a smile of approval.

"I don't know," Marina said, sizing up the innocent look Jack had on his face. "My husband looks sort of guilty to me."

5

"*H*ere's a table for your items," Kai said, her breath coming out in small clouds in the cool morning air. Despite Marina's concerns, she felt good about doing this for Holly. She rubbed her hands together and blew on them.

The only space left was a small table on the edge of the market.

The morning sun sparkled off tinsel garlands strung between market stalls, but this table was in a shaded, cold part of the market that didn't have as much traffic. Kai wished there had been a better spot, but space had been limited, and the holiday market filled up fast.

Nevertheless, Holly seemed grateful. "I don't know how to thank you for this. I was supposed to be in Los Angeles by now."

Kai took the top box from a stack they'd wheeled in with a dolly from Brooke's vehicle. She put it on the table. "This show isn't as large as the one you planned to do, but it's something. I hope you're not disappointed."

"It's not that. There's someone I hoped to meet there."

Now they were getting somewhere, Kai thought. "A boyfriend?"

"No, someone I want to find." Holly shook her head and placed her other boxes on the table. "It's not important. Who shall I pay for the space?"

Kai waved a hand to dismiss the offer. "Normally, that would be Cookie, who manages the farmers market and the new holiday market, but when she heard you were stranded, she comped your spot. It's the last one."

"She did that without even knowing me?"

"Well, you know me," Kai said brightly. "And that's practically the same thing."

A smile played on Holly's delicate features as she spread a metallic threaded cloth over the table. "So, I'm curious— why help a stranger like me?"

Kai shrugged. "I like to stay busy."

"Doesn't your baby keep you busy enough?"

"I like getting out and seeing people. And my husband is taking care of Stella today." Kai glanced around. "People are arriving now. I should help you set up."

When Holly agreed, Kai reached for a carton. Sometimes, it was easier to talk to strangers than friends, and Holly seemed receptive.

"For years, I performed with touring Broadway shows," Kai began. "I know what it feels like to land in a new city every few weeks. When I was on the road, I needed to see more than the inside of a theater or hotel room."

Holly nodded as she listened. "That sounds exciting, though I can see how it might get old. Were you homesick for Summer Beach?"

"Whenever I had time off, I stayed with Ginger. But I

was gone for months at a time." Kai spread a banner across the table. "How is this?"

"That looks nice, thanks." Holly angled her head. "How did you handle the traveling?"

Kai thought about that. "Between rehearsals and performances, I would slip away to explore the city. Small gestures meant a lot to me in that nomadic life. Maybe it was a cup of coffee served with a smile and a few words. Or a recommendation for a hidden bookstore or the best sushi. Each kindness made me feel a little less lonely. So, I figured you could use a friend for however long you're here."

"I'm glad you understand," Holly said, her voice thick with emotion. "This means a lot to me."

Kai reached up to flip the edge of the canopy back. Sunlight streamed in like a spotlight. "I don't think we need this overhead covering unless it rains. And let's angle the table for better viewing."

Christmas music drifted throughout the market, and Kai hummed along while positioning Holly's charming snow globes and glittering tree ornaments.

"Isn't that "Happy Holiday?" Holly asked.

"Sure is. It's from *Holiday Inn*, which was a 1942 movie and later, a musical." Kai grinned. "I have a weakness for old songs and show tunes."

"We all have our gifts."

"You sure do." Kai stepped back to admire their handiwork. "Your work is unique—and so beautifully crafted."

The young woman's ornaments glittered in the sunlight. Her snow globes held tiny, exquisite worlds within their crystal spheres.

Surveying the display, Holly clasped her hands. "This looks perfect, though I might be biased."

Kai noticed again how their visitor had an ethereal quality about her. She looked like a Christmas elf who'd wandered away from Santa's workshop and found herself on the beach.

"We Need a Little Christmas" began playing, and Kai hummed to the familiar refrain. She caught Holly watching her with amusement.

"And this one?"

"It's from *Mame*, another musical," Kai explained. She sang along to it.

When that song ended and another began, Kai said, "This is Judy Garland with "Have Yourself a Merry Little Christmas" from *Meet Me in St. Louis*. That was one of my long-running parts."

Holly adjusted an intricate ornament. "You love musical theater the way I love crafting."

"Stick around Summer Beach long enough, and I'll cast you as an elf in our community theater." Kai winked. "You've already got the look."

They were still laughing when a woman spied the display and hurried toward them. "Oh, my goodness, it's you. Holly from the Phoenix gift show."

Holly's eyes lit with recognition. "Beverly, it's so good to see you. What are you doing here?"

"I live in Summer Beach, and I can't believe you're here. I have to tell you something amazing." The other woman hugged her, emotion catching in her voice. "That ornament I bought from you last year, the one with the woman's face that looked so much like my mother's? Mom had passed away a few months earlier, so I hung it on my tree and...well, this might sound odd, but everything in my life changed after that. It was like having a piece of my mother with me. I keep it out all year now. It's my lucky talisman."

Beverly leaned in closer, her voice dropping to a whisper. "But here's the incredible part. My sister bought one of your ornaments too, and she just realized that the house painted on it is exactly like the one she bought here three months ago. She hadn't even seen the house when she bought the ornament. Isn't that wild?"

A blush crept across Holly's cheeks. "I just paint what I see," she murmured. "From memory, I mean."

Beverly looked perplexed. "But how could you have known?"

"I have a photographic memory for images," Holly added quickly. "If I see anything posted on social media, for example. Or in the newspaper. Maybe that's where I saw your mother's photo. The house might have been listed in the ad section."

"Maybe," Beverly said, inclining her head. "But what's truly remarkable is the impact your artwork has had on us. I can't explain it, but I feel such a rush of good feelings every time I touch the ornament."

A slow smile lifted Holly's lips. "That must be your mother's love. It will never leave you. Maybe you're just more aware of it now."

"I heard people use objects to focus attention," Beverly said. "Sort of like meditation."

Kai watched Holly carefully, Marina's concerns about her springing to mind.

Across the market, Brooke was arranging her organic produce, unaware of this extraordinary conversation. But this was so personal that Kai was hesitant to share it.

"Would you choose one for me?" Kai asked suddenly, surprising herself.

Holly studied her for a long moment, then reached for a snow globe, shook it, and handed it to Kai. "This one is for you."

Kai's fingers trembled as she took it. Crystalline snow swirled in lazy spirals, and when it settled, she gasped.

Inside the globe, a tiny figure in a familiar red dress sat at a piano with miniature sheet music scattered around her feet. A palm tree arched overhead, and an ocean wave curled beside it. But the piano was eerily reminiscent of one she knew.

Kai breathed out. "That piano looks like the one in Ginger's home. My mother taught me to play on it."

"Then it's yours," Holly said softly. "All my pieces eventually find their owners."

The snowflakes in the globe settled, but now Kai's world was shaken.

"How did you know?" she asked, but Holly was already helping Beverly find the right gifts for her daughters.

Kai lowered the snow globe. At once, she felt like she was seeing everything around her with heightened clarity.

The market sparkled with holiday decorations, but Kai suspected Holly could see what most people couldn't. That might be unnerving to many.

Maybe that's why Holly made up stories about her gift.

As Kai tucked the snow globe into her bag, she wondered if Holly could see what others hadn't seen *yet*.

Kai let out a breath. Marina was never going to believe this.

6

"*H*eather, dear, would you bring extra blankets for the beach bonfire?" Ginger asked, pulling on a pair of red leather gloves. "You'll find some in the study."

"Sure, I'll be just a moment," Heather replied.

While Heather gathered blankets, Ginger paused to admire her comfortable living room, now suffused with the glow of lights reflecting off the vintage ornaments her family had carefully hung on the tree. Heather had draped the mantel with decorative garlands, weaving them around family photos that chronicled years of love and laughter.

Ginger inhaled the fresh scent of evergreen boughs that Brooke had fashioned into a centerpiece for the table. It wasn't only the holiday decorations Ginger loved; more so, it was the family that gathered to help.

She checked her watch. They had ample time before sunset, but Heather and Cruise had to set up the food truck near the beach bonfire. While Blake wasn't working in the food truck, he was there to support Heather, manage the line, and ensure customers were happy.

Heather reappeared with an armful of soft throws. Her engagement ring twinkled in the light as she moved.

Blake appeared in the doorway. "The folding chairs are loaded onto the truck." He took the blankets from Heather as he spoke. "Ginger, are you sure you don't want to come with us? Cruise is driving, but we can squeeze you in."

"Oliver should be here shortly," Ginger replied. He'd asked that just the two of them go together to the bonfire tonight, which she found rather romantic. "I'll wait for him."

She adjusted the red cashmere scarf Bertrand had given her years ago. Quality lasted, and so did the love she still held in her heart for her husband, though he'd been gone many years.

"Okay, we'll see you there," Heather said. "I'll have two hot cups of cocoa for you."

After Heather and Blake left, Ginger walked to her window, watching the sun begin its descent over the Pacific. She touched the windowpane, now cool against her fingers.

She had the comforting sense that Bertrand approved of Oliver. Bertrand had enjoyed a long friendship with Oliver and his brother Kurt, who had been Ginger's first employer.

Yet, it was more than that. Sometimes, when Oliver arrived, she could almost hear Bertrand calling out to him. *What took you so long?* And then, his laughter seemed so real she had to smile, too.

The Christmas beach bonfire was an old tradition in Summer Beach, but this year was different. It might be the last one she would see, perhaps for a long time. That would depend on Oliver's decision—and hers, of course.

For now, she wanted to enjoy every moment.

The doorbell chimed, and Oliver stood on her porch, handsome as always in a red and black plaid flannel shirt and a down vest. His thick silver hair was slightly mussed, and his bright blue eyes sparkled with mischief.

Her heart warmed at the sight of him, though she wondered what he was up to. She loved being with him. This was a new chapter of her life, and Oliver Powell had arrived right on cue.

"Merry Christmas, darling." Oliver took her in his arms and kissed her. "Ready for some early festivities? I have a marvelous surprise for you."

"I'm more than ready." She leaned in to snuff out a candle on the table, but as she drew close to the flame, it sizzled and blazed, then flickered and snuffed itself out.

She and Oliver stared at the smoldering wick. "I didn't do that," she said slowly.

"Must be your natural magnetism," Oliver said. "Even fire is dazzled by your presence and bends to your indomitable will."

"If only I were that powerful," she said, somehow detecting a faint whiff of the pipe tobacco Bertrand favored. Maybe he was teasing her about her date with Oliver.

"Oh, but you are," Oliver said, running a hand over her shoulder. "I'm already in thrall to your charms."

"And I to yours, my darling." She drew her hand over his face, thinking how fortunate they'd reconnected. Beyond scientific explanations, life still held mysteries and surprises.

Perhaps most surprising of all was the relationship that

had blossomed with Oliver. Still marveling over their relationship, she chose a white wool jacket from the coat stand.

He held the jacket for her, helping her put it on. "Do you have everything, my dear?"

She glanced at the candle again, making sure the flame was out. "Everything I could possibly want."

Chuckling, Oliver opened the door for her. "Give it a moment. I don't think we'll ever run out of fresh ideas. That's what keeps us young at heart."

They walked outside, and she sucked in a breath of delight at a cherry-red Vespa parked in the drive. Silver tinsel and a red bow festooned the shiny scooter, and two matching helmets rested on the seats. "Is this yours?"

"No, it's yours. Merry Christmas, sweetheart." A broad grin filled Oliver's face, and his eyes twinkled. "Won't it be fun spinning around town on this?"

"Oh, my goodness, I thought you were joking a couple of months ago when we talked about scooters." She flung her arms around Oliver and peppered him with joyful kisses.

Laughing, Oliver kissed her back before handing her a helmet. "You should know by now that I take fun quite seriously. Let's see what you can do with this beauty."

Ginger hesitated, but only for a moment. She recalled how fearlessly she'd driven her scooter years ago. She slid the helmet over her hair while he did the same.

They adjusted the straps, grinning at each other.

She perched on the seat with Oliver behind her. "I never thought I'd be whizzing around on a Vespa again. Why, I haven't been on one since Paris. I hope I don't fall off."

"You won't. You rise to every occasion, Ginger

Delavie." As she started the engine, he pressed his hand against her shoulder. "I remember visiting you and Bertrand in Paris and watching you zip along the Champs-Élysées on your scooter, your paisley scarf flowing in the breeze, turning heads in your wake. What a sight you were. And still are."

She eased the scooter forward, surprised that she felt so comfortable on it. "Well, I'll be. I haven't lost my touch. Rather like solving a quadratic equation—one never forgets." She lifted her chin. "Climb on. I promise not to kill you."

Chuckling, Oliver sat behind her, his strong arms encircling and anchoring her.

With the fresh wind on her face and her red scarf trailing behind her, Ginger steered away from the cottage, filled with exhilaration. The short trip to the beach bonfire lasted only a few minutes.

"You can use this scooter almost anywhere," Oliver said as Ginger approached the Coral Cafe food truck. "It's easy to park and faster than walking."

Excitement sparked through her. "Such fun, too. I love it, dear." She appreciated his thoughtfulness and playful nature more than mere words could express. "It's perfect to continue this grand adventure we're on."

"So grand it is," Oliver echoed, raising his voice against the rush of the ocean as they neared the shoreline again. "Are you ready for our trip next month?"

"I love Boston in the snow. It will be wonderful to meet your nephew again. I haven't seen him since he was a child."

With the breeze squeezing moisture from her eyes, she wondered, would they stay there? It seemed neither of them were ready to commit just yet. If Oliver were to leave and she stayed here, she wanted him to remember how they were. The painting spoke what she might not find the words to say.

Oliver leaned in as if reading her mind, his breath warm against her neck. "We don't have to make any decision just yet."

When she pulled alongside the holiday-decorated food truck, Heather and Blake stared in astonishment.

Cruise stepped from inside, grinning and giving her a double thumbs-up. "Looking good, Ginger."

"Let me help you, sweetheart." Oliver hopped off. "I always open your door, and this is no exception."

Laughing, Ginger extended her hand like a queen, and Oliver helped her descend from the scooter while a crowd gathered around them, remarking on the shiny scooter.

She removed her helmet, fluffed her ginger-tinted hair, and turned to Heather. "What do you think?"

"Wow, it's so sassy," Heather said, laughing. "Whose is it?"

"Mine. Dear Oliver surprised me with an early Christmas gift." She posed beside it.

"Wait until Mom sees you on this," Heather replied, snapping a photo. "It's so cool. I want one, too."

Blake looked impressed and gave Ginger a high-five. "They're a blast to ride, and you handle it well."

Ginger appreciated that. "I rode one all over Paris back in the day."

They stashed their helmets in the food truck before greeting friends who commented and inspected the new Vespa.

Ginger loved the attention. She leaned over to whisper

in Oliver's ear. "This is one of the most amazing gifts I've ever received. I never dreamed of it, but it's perfect for me. Thank you, darling."

With his arm around her, Oliver beamed. "It makes me happy that you like it. It just arrived, and I couldn't wait until Christmas to give it to you." He kissed her cheek. "Let's join the crowd."

The bonfire was already flaming on the beach, snapping and crackling. Stars were flickering to life, and people laughed and talked as they shared homemade sweets and hot thermoses. Ginger inhaled deeply. The sweet aroma of hot cocoa blended with the smell of the bonfire was intoxicating.

She savored every moment of the merriment around her. *This is Christmas at the beach*, she thought, marking the memory.

Oliver squeezed her hand. "Are you ready for a peppermint hot cocoa? I hear the Coral Cafe food truck makes pretty good ones."

"That sounds divine," Ginger replied. "They're based on my original recipe, so I can vouch for them."

"Two special ones, coming right up," Heather said. "How about a slice of hot gingerbread to go with that? Cruise just took some from the oven."

"Why not?" Ginger replied, smiling.

A few minutes later, she and Oliver strolled through the crowd, enjoying their warm drinks while greeting friends. They spoke to Leilani and Roy Miyake, who owned the Hidden Garden nursery. They said hello to Mayor Bennett Dylan, and Ginger saw her friend April Raines with her family, who now lived on nearby Crown Island.

Marina waved at them near the fire, where she sat with

Jack and Leo. Vanessa was there too, chatting with her friends Denise and John, while their daughter Samantha roasted marshmallows with Leo under Jack's supervision.

"Are you okay?" Marina asked. "Heather just sent me a photo of you with a helmet and a Vespa."

"Why wouldn't I be? I love my new Christmas gift." Ginger squeezed Oliver's hand. "And I adore this lovely man for it. We had such fun riding it here. I plan to use it around town." Or wherever they might end up, she added silently to herself.

Kai and Axe swayed near the fire with little Stella, still wide awake and transfixed by Axe's friends singing carols. Their harmonies carried on the evening breeze, along with the sound of waves and children's laughter.

Brooke and Chip also sat with them, though their three older boys played tag with other kids near the water. Clover, their newest addition, slept bundled against Brooke's chest.

"What a perfect evening," Ginger said to Marina while Jack drew Oliver into a conversation.

"Where is your house guest?" Marina asked.

"Holly left earlier but promised she would be here." Ginger peered around. "There she is, with Shelly by the food truck." Ivy's sister held the hand of a squirming toddler—little Daisy, Ginger recalled. How their family and those of their friends had grown. She watched them with satisfaction.

Holly's laughter carried across the beach. The young woman seemed to blend into the community, bringing joy wherever she went. She had relaxed in the last few days, but Ginger still sensed a nervous energy about her.

"She looks happy here." Ginger let out a small sigh. "I wish she didn't have to leave Summer Beach."

Marina gazed after her. "So do I. She seems to need a home, and we have a nice art community she could be part of."

"I sensed your concern when she arrived."

"We all look out for you." Marina paused as if holding back. "Maybe I was being overprotective."

"You thought I was losing my judgment, didn't you?" When Marina looked sheepish, Ginger sniffed. "I assure you, I'm as sharp as ever."

"I'm sorry," Marina murmured, blushing. "I know you're perfectly capable of looking out for yourself."

"I've been doing that a long time, but you're forgiven. It's Christmas, after all." Ginger glanced at Holly again. For some reason, she felt the young woman had a place here. "As for Holly, some people have gifts we don't fully understand. Beyond science and logic lay intuition, faith, and love."

"And second sight?" Marina added, leaning forward. "Kai told me about what happened at the market with a woman Holly knew."

As Marina shared Kai's story, Ginger nodded thoughtfully, staring into the fire as flames danced, sending up a shower of golden sparks. "Have you ever known something in your heart you couldn't explain?"

"Sometimes I have gut instincts, especially about my children."

"There you are then," Ginger said as if that finished the conversation. "Different levels of intuition exist. Some might think it magical, though it's likely a phenomenon that's not fully understood."

Although Marina appeared satisfied with this explanation, Ginger sensed this story was far from over.

*a*s the evening temperature dropped, everyone drew closer to the bonfire. Suddenly, sleigh bells jingled in the darkness beyond the reach of the fire's glow. Children's eyes rounded at the sound, and excitement swept across the crowd.

Marina peered down the beach. "I think we have another surprise tonight."

This is what the men had been whispering about earlier. Jack, Axe, and Chip had disappeared a few minutes ago to help.

Kai had left Stella with Brooke, so she was clearly involved with this annual visit. Likely, she was the head costumer.

Leo and Samantha looked up from their toasted marshmallows, heads turning toward the sound as the *a cappella* singers wrapped up a rousing rendition of *Jingle Bells*, a preview of the holiday choral show they were giving at the Shell Amphitheater.

Drawing nearer was a beach rescue vehicle outfitted like a sleigh. And at the wheel—

"Look, it's Santa," Leo yelled.

"With his trusty sidekick, too," Marina added, laughing.

Scout rode in the passenger seat, a sparkly red collar fastened around his furry ruff, his tongue lolling in a grin.

"That dog is living his best life," Ginger said, chuckling.

Axe's friends began singing "Here Comes Santa Claus," and soon everyone joined in. The fire crackled higher, sending sparks to the stars.

As the vehicle pulled up, Marina smiled at the beach-meets-Christmas decorations. A life preserver was wrapped with ribbons, and a first aid kit sported a big bow.

"Ho, ho, ho!" A deep voice rolled across the beach like thunder.

Suddenly, Marina was surprised. "That's not Jack," she whispered to Ginger and Kai, who had rejoined them.

Every year, the men took turns playing the jolly St. Nick. Although it was supposed to be a secret until Santa arrived, Jack had been dropping hints, complaining about fake beards being scratchy.

Marina shot to her feet. "Wait, who *is* that?"

Kai giggled. "I know."

"So do I," Heather cried. She could hardly contain her enthusiasm.

"It couldn't be, could it?" Marina hardly dared to hope. When the vehicle stopped, Santa disembarked. She'd recognize that youthful swagger anywhere. The children raced toward the truck, and she pressed a hand to her chest and screamed. "It is! It's—"

"Mom, shush. The kids!" Heather exploded with laughter.

Kai took Marina's hands, jumping with excitement with her and Heather. "Don't let on that you know. He has to stay in character."

Santa waved at Marina with a wink.

Just then, Jack swung off the back of the vehicle, grinning broadly. He made his way toward her.

She flung her arms around him. "I thought his schedule was full."

"It is," Jack said, taking her in his arms. "But as it turned out, he's not too busy to visit his mother."

Leo tugged his father's jacket. "Hey, Dad, is that who you picked up at the airport?"

"That's right. It was top secret, kiddo."

"And you didn't tell me?" Marina jabbed him in the chest. "Why not?"

"And spoil your Christmas surprise?" Jack kissed her. "This was your heart's desire, and I couldn't think of anything else that would mean as much. Merry Christmas, darling. Hope you don't mind getting your gift a little early."

Tears sprang to her eyes, and Marina wiped them away, smiling. Having Ethan home for the holidays was all she'd wished for. "Oh, thank you, darling. But I still don't know how you managed it."

"That's my secret," Jack said, his eyes sparkling.

"Jack found a special flight, booked his ticket, and arranged everything," Kai gushed.

Marina turned to her sister. "Did you know about this?"

"Not until I had to apply his beard and fit his costume. I was as surprised as you are." Kai grinned. "I had to use extra padding—that kid has some serious abs now."

When Santa opened a bag of candy, Leo and Samantha

followed the younger children. Brooke's sons—Alder, Rowan, and Oakley—joined them, too.

"Well, what do we have here?" Santa boomed, settling into a lawn chair Blake had quickly placed near the fire. "It seems I've found all the good girls and boys of Summer Beach. Gather round, everyone."

Ethan's gray-blue eyes glittered beneath bushy white eyebrows, and he winked at Marina.

"I never would have imagined," she said, blowing a kiss at him. "I can hardly wait to hear how he's doing."

Jack put his arm around her. "Soon. He has a very important job to do first."

Oliver leaned close to Ginger. "Did you have any idea about this?"

"No more than Marina," Ginger said, touching her heart. "What a thoughtful gesture."

Oliver winked at Jack. "I knew you had it in you. This is far better than your other idea."

"What are you two talking about?" Kai asked, looking at them suspiciously.

"Just guy stuff," Jack said, chuckling.

With her husband's arm around her, Marina watched as Ethan produced candy canes with a flourish, passing them around. He continued his performance, making each child feel special.

A happy thought dawned on her: This was Summer Beach at its holiday finest. Where real magic could happen on a winter beach, where a golfer could become Santa Claus, where family meant more than blood, and where love, like the tides, could sweep in and transform everything.

Still watching her son, Marina sighed happily. "He's such a natural in this role."

"I coached him a little," Kai said, folding her arms. "He needed a few lines besides *ho, ho, ho.*"

Soon, helper elves brought bags to Santa's side and began to pass out gifts to the children: Frisbees, floaties, volleyballs, and beach toys for sandcastle building. Santa posed with the children as their parents took photos.

"Oh, my gosh, I have to get a photo of Stella up there with Cousin Santa," Kai said, waving to Brooke, who was holding Clover. "Let's go."

Marina couldn't imagine a more perfect Christmas bonfire. Her sisters took their little ones to stand in line with other parents. When it was their turn, they hammed it up with Santa, and everyone laughed.

After taking photos and giving gifts to the children, Santa motioned for them to join him. "And what about you, Heather? Have you been good this year?"

"You know I have been," Heather said, punching her brother playfully in the arm. "I have to return to the food truck, but I'll see you later. If you stay at the cottage, don't walk around in your underwear, Santa. Ginger has another guest."

"Oh, yeah? Who?"

"Another elf named Holly." Heather grinned, clearly relishing teasing him. "You'll meet her soon enough."

Marina was next, playing along. "Santa, I don't suppose you have any pro golfers in that bag of yours?"

"You're in luck. There's one left." He wrapped his arms around Marina. "Merry Christmas, Mom. Were you surprised?"

"Completely," she replied, hugging her son. "I'm so happy to see you."

A few minutes later, Marina stood with her family, waving goodbye to Santa as he drove his sleigh away into the night.

While the bonfire burned brightly, Marina enjoyed being with her family and friends. They continued to celebrate, bound together by love and the magic of Christmas by the sea.

"Happy?" Ginger asked, leaning in.

Marina clasped her hands. "Beyond happy. Completely fulfilled. Everyone I love is here now."

Although Marina had welcomed Oliver into their family, she fervently hoped this wouldn't be the last year Ginger would spend with them here.

But if it was, it was perfect.

8

"*T*hanks for managing the cafe today," Marina said to Cruise, who would cook while a reliable part-timer would wait tables. "All the prep work is complete, and the holiday menu is fairly streamlined."

"No worries," he replied, gesturing toward only a few tables occupied for breakfast. "It will be slow today. Most people are shopping for gifts."

"I'll be back for dinner," she said with a wave. They were also closing a little earlier.

Marina strolled along the winding pathway from the cafe to Ginger's cottage, eager to talk to Ethan. She entered the kitchen, where she saw her grandmother seated at the red Formica table, sipping coffee and reading the Summer Beach bulletin.

"Good morning, darling," Ginger said, lowering the newspaper.

"Is anyone else up?"

"Not yet. The kids came home late from the bonfire last night, and then they stayed up and talked by the fireplace."

"This is the first time Heather and Ethan have been separated for any length of time. They probably had a lot to talk about."

Ginger removed her reading glasses. "Holly was with them, too."

As much as Ginger's guest was growing on her, Marina was slightly concerned. "I hope Heather and Ethan still had a chance to catch-up."

"It sounded like they were all having a good time." A smile touched Ginger's lips. "There was a lot of laughter floating up the stairs last night. I wouldn't worry about them. They're all adults now."

Marina sighed and nodded. "When did that happen? It seems like yesterday they were still in grammar school."

A commotion broke out upstairs, with Ethan yelling and Heather screaming with laughter. A door slammed, and Heather raced downstairs in her pajamas. Her long hair was still sleep-tousled.

"Hey, Mom. I didn't hear you come in." Still grinning, Heather hugged Marina and made straight for the coffeemaker.

"What happened up there?" Marina asked, amused at their antics.

Heather shrugged. "I woke up Ethan, that's all. He's gotten lazy."

Marina shot a look at Ginger. "And how exactly did you wake him?"

"She bounced onto my bed and attacked me." Ethan glared at his sister from the doorway. He still wore his pajama bottoms with a T-shirt.

"You can't handle a little tickling like you used to do to

me?" Heather poured two cups and handed one to her brother. "Here you go, grumpy Santa."

Marina chuckled; things hadn't changed between them. "Who is hungry?"

Ethan rubbed his face. "Starving, Mom."

"As usual." Marina glanced at Ginger. "Mind if I whip up breakfast?"

"Please. I love watching you cook. You'll find plenty of eggs in the refrigerator."

"Can you make one of your special omelets with biscuits, Mom? I miss those."

"Wow, Ethan, you get special treatment," Heather teased.

Marina picked up on that. "He's going to help me right after he changes, aren't you? We have a guest in the house."

With a groan, Ethan charged upstairs, and Heather raced after him. Minutes later, they reappeared in sweatshirts and jeans, their dark blond hair looking a little less wild. Ethan's frame was trimmer but more muscular, and the freckles that appeared in the sun were prominent across his nose now.

Marina whisked eggs in a bowl while Ethan brought out the dry ingredients—flour, butter, and milk. Minutes later, fluffy Southern-style biscuits were baking in the old O'Keefe & Merritt fire-engine red oven.

Heather hip-checked her brother as she reached for berries. "Are you sure those carbs are on your golf pro diet?"

Ethan made a face. "I'm on holiday, and it's none of your business."

"These two haven't missed a beat," Ginger said, laughing at their behavior.

Marina kept an eye on the oven. When the biscuits were ready, she pulled them out, and a heavenly scent filled the air.

"Good morning," came a soft voice. Holly appeared in the doorway wearing a sweater and jeans.

Ethan froze mid-reach for a hot biscuit and butter. His eyes followed Holly as she sat at the table across from Ginger. "Did you sleep well?" he asked.

"Until some sort of commotion woke me," she replied, grinning.

Across the room, Ginger caught Marina's eye and raised an eyebrow.

Marina picked up on an unusual tone in her son's voice. Was he interested in Holly or just flirting? Darting a glance at him, she decided it was likely an innocent holiday crush. She slid omelets from a pair of pans and started two more.

"That was your fault for not getting up right away," Heather told Ethan.

"You can't expect me to be coherent from a dead sleep," Ethan protested, then turned to Holly with interest brightening his face. "I meant to ask you about the ornaments and snow globes you make last night. Kai told me about them."

"They all sold out at the market," Holly said, accepting the mug of coffee Marina offered. "Almost all, that is. I kept a few special ones back."

Holly's phone buzzed in her pocket, and she took it out. "That's the garage. Looks like my car will be ready later this afternoon." With a small sigh, Holly wrapped her hands around her mug. "I should head to Los Angeles then."

"Must you leave so soon?" Ginger asked. "We're going to Beach Waves, a salon in the village, for a little holiday pampering. I've already booked us all in—you too, Holly. We're meeting Kai there, too."

"For her pink and purple highlights," Marina added, serving omelets to Ginger and Holly first.

"I could come along," Ethan said eagerly.

"Down, boy," Heather teased. "It's girls only. Besides, your hair's perfect. Looks like you just had it cut."

"You could stay another night," Ethan suggested to Holly, ignoring his sister's remark. "Leave tomorrow instead? You shouldn't drive in the dark."

Holly sipped her coffee, considering. "Maybe..."

"What's waiting in L.A.?" Marina asked, keeping her tone casual. "The craft show there is over, isn't it?"

Holly's voice grew quiet. "There's someone I'd hoped to see before Christmas."

"Boyfriend?" Ethan asked, leaning forward.

Smiling, Holly shook her head. "I'm not dating anyone."

Ethan looked pleased by that. "Family?"

Marina shot him a warning look. "Holly grew up like your Grandpa Dennis," she said lightly. She plated two more omelets for the twins.

"Oh, I get it." Ethan's gaze softened as he realized what that meant. "That's cool. You're like us."

Heather reached across the table and squeezed Holly's hand. "Welcome to the complicated family club. We've got T-shirts."

Holly's laughter bubbled up and seemed to surprise even herself. "I'll join you at the salon. The person I'm meeting has a lot of style. I want to make a good first impression. It's important..." Her voice trailed off.

"Sounds mysterious," Ethan said, waggling his eyebrows. "So it's settled. You'll stay tonight."

"Just one more night, if that's okay."

"Of course it is," Ginger said. "However, we should go soon. We don't want to be late and lose our appointments."

Ethan wolfed down his breakfast. "I'll see you all later."

Marina watched Ethan rush upstairs. Beside her, Ginger murmured, "I'll bet he finds an excuse to stop by Beach Waves."

AFTER ARRIVING AT THE SALON, Marina opened the door for their party. The bell on the salon's front door jingled, matching everyone's high spirits.

Kai was already waiting for them. "Hi, you gorgeous ladies—who are about to look even more fabulous shortly. It seems Ginger booked every stylist here for us."

Holly glanced around the bustling salon, splashed in shades of pink and whimsical sayings on the walls. "What a cute place."

Ginger spoke to the receptionist. "There are several of us, but I would like our guest to have special treatment. It's a big day for her tomorrow."

"I understand," the receptionist said brightly. "Brandy can take her right now."

At the mention of the owner's name, Holly swung around, suddenly alert. "Did you say, Brandy?"

A woman a little older than Holly turned around to greet her. "Welcome to Beach Waves."

Suddenly, Holly looked flustered, and her face paled as she stared at the salon owner. "*You're* Brandy?"

Nodding, Brandy looked surprised at Holly's tone. "Are you okay?"

"I think I need some water," Holly said, sinking into a chair. "I'm feeling like I might faint."

"I'll get you a glass," Brandy said, frowning with concern. She hurried away.

Kai sat next to Holly and took her hand. "What was that about? Do you know Brandy?"

Looking panicked, Holly blurted out in a hoarse whisper, "That's who I wanted to try to meet in Los Angeles. What is she doing *here*?"

"This is her salon," Kai said. "But she moved from L.A. What's going on with you?"

Holly pressed a hand to her heart. "It's complicated. Not long ago, I took a DNA test and got a match."

Marina knelt beside the young woman. "On Brandy?"

Dabbing her eyes, Holly nodded. "I think she's…my sister," she finished softly. "But I don't think she knows that. I wasn't even sure if I was going to talk to her. I just wanted to see what she looked like."

"Well, you're here now," Kai said.

"But I'm not ready yet." Holly bit her lip and frowned. "It wasn't supposed to be like this."

9

*G*inger placed a hand on Holly's shoulder to comfort her. "Life seldom serves up what we expect, dear." She traded a look with Marina, who nodded. This was a delicate matter of importance to these two young women.

Now Ginger understood why fate had drawn Holly here. She was as sure of this as when telling her life story to Jack. Coincidences had figured prominently in her life and likely in most others, if people thought about it. Holly's intuitive sense was strong; whether she realized it or not, she was meant to be in Summer Beach.

"We're here with you, so it's a perfect time," Marina said, taking her hand. "One of us can talk to Brandy for you, or with you."

Holly searched Ginger's face. "After collapsing like this, I guess I should tell her now, right?"

"That would be best," Ginger replied.

When Brandy returned with the water, Ginger rose and took her to one side. "Is there somewhere we can talk privately? It seems our friend has some information for you."

"Sure." Brandy furrowed her brow with concern. "I have a small office in the back." She led the way.

Ginger clasped Holly's hand. "Marina and Kai, you two should get started with your stylists. They're on a schedule." With Holly beside her, she followed Brandy.

Brandy opened the door and showed them into the small room. She leaned on the edge of a desk that held a computer, stacks of paperwork, and professional magazines dedicated to haircare and wellness.

"You seem shaken," Brandy said, inclining her head. "Should we call a doctor for you?"

Holly shook her head. She seemed to struggle to find her words.

"Then what's this all about?" Brandy asked.

Ginger put her arm around the younger woman. "Holly is a very special, talented young woman that anyone would be lucky to have in their family. Being naturally curious, Holly took a DNA test."

"Wait a minute." Brandy's lips parted, and her entire demeanor shifted as she leaned forward. "Are you *that* Holly? My sister?"

"I-I think so," Holly replied, looking shocked at Brandy's knowledge. "I mean, I'm pretty sure, if you trust DNA." She drew in her lower lip, looking hopeful.

Brandy let out a little cry and clasped a hand to her mouth. "Oh, my goodness, it's really you." Her eyes glistened with tears. "You look just like our mom. I've always wondered where you were and if you were okay. You were just a baby when everything happened."

Brandy held her arms wide, and Holly fell into her embrace. Both women cried with joy.

"Who would have thought?" Ginger said happily, choking with emotion as well.

Watching these two lovely young women reunite, she sent up a silent prayer of appreciation. Unwittingly, she had also played a part, she realized. What if she hadn't asked Holly to stay with her? None of this might have happened.

Listening to them, Ginger pieced together the story as it tumbled out. They had different fathers who both disappeared, and their mother had a severe nervous breakdown. Unable to care for her young daughters, she relinquished control of them. The sisters were split apart, with both going into foster care.

"Eventually, I was adopted," Brandy said. "You were barely a year old, so you wouldn't have known I existed, but I remembered you. I tried to find you once, but they said you'd left foster care with no forwarding address. Since we had different last names, it was like people forgot we were related."

"I always felt like I belonged somewhere else," Holly said.

"You belong with me now," Brandy said. "Where are you living?"

Holly explained that she lived with different friends and traveled the market circuit for arts and crafts. "I can hardly believe I found you in Summer Beach. I thought you were in Los Angeles. I was on my way there when my car broke down."

"This is where we lived as a family," Brandy said. "That's why I returned to Summer Beach. I thought if you ever looked for me, you might start here. Besides, it's such a sweet town with the kindest people. Like Ginger."

"So I have been here before," Holly said in awe, turning to Ginger. "How could I have remembered?"

"The mind and memory are more powerful than we know," Ginger said, embracing the two young women. "What a wonderful second chance life has given you."

"This is the best Christmas gift I could have imagined," Brandy said. "Now, I want to pamper my sister. You're going to have the works today—whatever you want." She clasped Holly's hands. "Stay with me, too. I have a guest bedroom that can be yours for as long as you want. Forever, I hope. We have so much to talk about."

Ginger nodded at Holly. "I've loved having you in my home. But this is the season for catching up with family."

As she watched the two women walk arm in arm from the office, Ginger marveled at the synchronicity of life.

And who knew? Maybe Ethan and Holly were meant to meet this Christmas as well. Ginger smiled and closed the door behind her.

This was the way of things in Summer Beach. New faces arrived to open new chapters of life, while others left for adventures. Life here was like the ebb and flow of the ocean, ever changing, always in motion.

Ginger could hardly wait to see Oliver this evening to tell him what had happened.

10

*G*inger tucked her hand through the crook of Oliver's arm as they walked along Main Street, admiring the holiday decorations.

Dusk settled over the village. Along the street, holiday lights twinkled in shop windows, and tiny white lights encircled the graceful sterns, or trunks, of palm trees and outlined their fronds. Tomorrow was Christmas Eve.

"Was that the last of your holiday shopping?" she asked after they left the travel agency. Oliver had asked her to help him choose a gift for his nephew and family. He'd once mentioned they dreamed of taking their children on a celebrity mouse-themed cruise out of Florida. With her help, he decided on a gift package for that from Get Away Travel.

"Most of my shopping is complete," Oliver replied, studying her. "For the last hour, I've been trying to place what is different about you."

"Brandy gave me a new hairstyle." Ginger told him about the visit to the salon. "I had planned to pamper

Marina, Kai, and Heather—Brooke cares little for such things—but I never imagined it would be such an emotional day."

"How so?" he asked with interest.

"I included Holly," she said. "She came away with an updated style and a new-found sister." She told him about what had transpired between her house guest and Brandy. "She returned home with Heather to pack her bag and pick up her car. This will be her first Christmas spent with a real family member."

"That's remarkable," Oliver said. "I'm glad for her. Being near family is important."

All around them, Christmas lights flickered on. In the distance, the lights of her beloved Coral Cottage glowed against the deepening blue of the ocean. Her heart fluttered at the familiar sight.

Oliver's step slowed. "I've been thinking about our families." His voice carried a gentle gravity. "And about how much I enjoy Summer Beach. It's grown on me."

Ginger squeezed his arm. "I hoped it would."

"The weather's quite pleasant," he mused, his eyes twinkling. "And the golfing is exceptional."

"Many communities offer that."

"And you know how much I care for you." His voice softened. "Would you consider spending more time together?"

"Can you be more precise, my dear?"

Oliver smiled. "How about the rest of our lives and wherever life takes us?"

"That's a broad question. Does this have to do with your nephew?"

Nodding, Oliver said, "Chris isn't letting up. He still

wants me to move near him. For some reason, he thinks I'll suddenly wake up as an infirm, crotchety old man one day."

"In theory, anything could happen," Ginger said, understanding his nephew's concern. "Although I hope your lovely nature doesn't fail you."

Oliver chuckled at that. "Chris is family. He's like the child we never had. But I must consider you, too," he added firmly. He stopped near Spirits & Vine, where an Ella Fitzgerald song was playing, "Have Yourself a Merry Little Christmas." He gestured toward the entryway. "That's one of your favorites, as I recall. Care for a hot toddy?"

She sensed he wanted to talk away from her family. And so did she. "They serve mulled wine for the holidays. Let's go in."

They sat at a table near a crackling fireplace, and the server brought two cups of warm, mulled wine. "I'm torn, Ginger. Plain and simple. I've always loved Boston, and we could have a good life there."

Ginger stirred her toddy with a cinnamon stick thoughtfully before setting it aside. "We can have a great life wherever we are. Even the markets of Marrakech or the wilds of the Serengeti."

"You remembered," he said, surprised.

"I have an excellent memory for what's important. And so do you." He had only mentioned those bucket list items once, but that's all it took for her.

"I count myself lucky to be in that category. And I haven't forgotten that little patisserie in Paris by the U.S. Embassy. I can almost taste the *pain au chocolat*." Oliver leaned closer to her. "There is still so much I want to do and experience with you. Still, we should be responsible. At what point do we plan for our inevitable future?"

She stroked his hand, pleased he'd also remembered what was on her list. "Who says what is inevitable? I've found that most of what we worry about never comes to pass. The best plans are fluid, leaving room for enjoyment, regardless."

"I suppose I would agree." He sipped his wine and stared into the dancing flames. "What if I'm not ready for that move yet? Does that sound selfish?"

"Not at all. It's your life to live."

"Or, we could be bi-coastal for a while."

Ginger knew she would have decisions to make, too. She had a life to live as well. "Let's visit your nephew with an open mind, shall we?"

He studied the table for a moment. "I know we've talked around the subject for a while, but would you consider moving to Boston with me?"

"That depends on the offer."

Oliver grinned. "That was presumptuous of me, wasn't it?"

"Premature, I'd say," she said, kissing him by the warmth of the fire.

He gazed at her with love and admiration in his eyes. "Airplanes fly both ways, don't they?"

"Indeed they do."

As they sat comfortably with each other, Ginger's mind wandered to her beloved Coral Cottage. The house had been her husband's wedding gift to her and was filled with a lifetime of memories. Raising their daughter, welcoming grandchildren and great-grandchildren, and hosting countless friends and gatherings. And now the walls rang with Oliver's laughter, the hearth warmed with their love.

Still, it was only a structure that could be reduced to rubble by a spark or a tsunami. Even loved ones came and went from this earthly existence. Time was theirs to appreciate in the moment.

"Maybe there's another option," Oliver said slowly, his eyes sparkling.

"What do you have in mind?" She reached for his hand again. "Backpacking or sailing around the world together? I have friends doing just that now."

"Somewhere we can use a shiny red Vespa."

Oliver smiled that smile she'd grown to love, the one that promised delightful surprises. "Any hints you can share?"

"Now that would be classified information."

Ginger laughed, recognizing her phrase turned back to her. Oliver was intriguing, teasing her with possibilities.

As always, she was up for it.

Laughter rang out from a nearby table, and they turned. Jack was there with his brothers-in-law, Chip and Axe. They were huddled around the table as if sharing secrets.

"Looks like we're no longer alone," Ginger said, smiling. "This is a small town; I'm surprised we've had this much time to ourselves."

"Excuse me for a moment," Oliver said. "I need to speak to them about something. Do you mind waiting?"

Ginger rested her chin on her hand, feigning exasperation. "You're full of secrets today, aren't you?"

Grinning, Oliver kissed her cheek. "'Tis the season, my love. All will be revealed in time."

"Go if you must, then. I'm an independent woman." She laughed and shooed him away.

This Christmas, she had secrets of her own.

She watched the men huddling like a sports team. Axe looked like the head coach, speaking in hushed tones and motioning to the others. Blake was there, too. Oliver appeared to chime in with suggestions.

He got along well with her granddaughter's husbands and the younger generation of Ethan, Leo, and Brooke's boys.

She wondered what they had in mind. Whatever it was, they looked excited.

When Oliver returned, he wore an expression of delight. He scooted his chair closer to her. "Will you promise me one thing?"

"Let's hear it first."

"You never saw anything today. None of them were here," he added, nodding toward the other men. "I don't want to spoil the surprise. And I know how good you are at protecting important, top-secret projects."

"I have no idea what you're talking about," she said with a shrug. "I haven't seen anything interesting here— except for you, my dear."

"Thank you for that. It will be worth it, I promise." Oliver kissed her hand. "Tomorrow, we're all planning to golf early in the day."

Ginger laughed at his attempt. "You're a lousy liar," she whispered with a conspiratorial wink. "But I choose to believe you this time. Just so you know."

11

"Have you heard from Oliver today?" Marina asked as she mixed pureed pumpkin into cream cheese. "I've been trying to reach Jack, but he's not picking up his phone. That's not like him, so I suspect something."

"Oliver checked in this morning," Ginger said. "I imagine he's out shopping." She removed a pair of springform pans lined with a mixture of crumbled graham crackers and ginger cookies from the hot oven.

Marina made a face. "Golfing was Jack's excuse, but he forgot his clubs in the garage."

Heather turned around from her cookie station in Ginger's kitchen. "Blake said he was meeting Jack and Ethan."

"Well, don't look at me," Kai said when they turned to her. "Axe went to work. He has a project that's run into trouble. Those custom home clients on the ridgetop can be awfully demanding." She paused to tickle Stella's little face.

"On Christmas Eve?" Marina lifted an eyebrow.

"Where's your sense of holiday distrust? They're up to something."

"Let them be," Ginger said, smiling. "They're probably on a last-minute shopping spree. You know how some men are."

"They'd better be back before the show tonight," Kai said, arranging shaped dough on a cookie sheet. "I'm not going to disrespect the performers by traipsing in late at the Shell on Christmas Eve. Axe reserved a section for all of us in the front."

"Everyone in town is talking about the holiday choral performance," Ginger said. "I know you'd love to be on stage, but you made a good choice this year."

"How can such a tiny creature take over your world— not to mention the laundry? Still, I wouldn't trade her for all the starring roles." Kai kissed Stella in her baby carrier, and the little girl cooed and smiled. "She's such an angel today. I hope she'll take a long nap while we finish baking."

Ginger tested the butternut squash soup simmering on the back burner of her stove. "How is your menu shaping up?"

"I've done most of the prep work," Marina said.

The last few days had been a whir of shopping and preparations. She had used the cafe's kitchen for most of her prep work. Her large refrigerators were convenient to hold feasts such as this.

She ticked off her menu from memory. "Beef Wellington, roast duck, honey glazed salmon, and a vegetarian lasagna are the main courses. We can nibble on crudité, glazed nuts, oysters Rockefeller, and shrimp cocktail. And for tonight, we'll have the Christmas tamales that Rosa delivered."

Heather looked up. "Blake's mom is bringing an assortment of imported cheeses and caviar. Arlette has fancy tastes."

"Nothing wrong with that," Ginger said. "Why, the foie gras in Paris on Christmas was such a treat with champagne." She sighed at the memory. "And what about side dishes?"

"I'll serve the classics," Marina replied. "Pureed potatoes and roasted brussels sprouts. Jack will grill Brooke's fresh vegetables. We'll also have a crisp endive, apple, and walnut salad. And your butternut squash soup."

"Get to the good stuff," Kai said. "Dessert, please."

Marina laughed. "Ginger and I have made a traditional Yule log, a *bûche de Noël*." She swept her hand over the cheesecake filling ready to pour into the round springform pans. "Cheesecakes, obviously. One pumpkin and one with cherries."

"Aunt Brooke mentioned chocolate mousse," Heather said.

"That's Brooke's specialty." Marina picked up a spatula. "She makes hers with dark chocolate and silken tofu. It's delicious and no one ever guesses."

"The cookies for the kids are almost ready," Kai added. "Bells, stars, and tree shapes. Along with these delicious gingerbread girls and boys." She bit the head of a gingerbread figure. "Delicious."

"Leave some for the children," Ginger said, smiling.

"I will, but I get Stella's share until her teeth come in." Kai tapped her baby's nose. "We have a deal, don't we, boo-boo?"

Marina glanced around, pleased with their efforts. The soup and appetizers would hold everyone over until after the show. "When the performance is over, I'll hurry to the cafe to set up the buffet, tamales, and desserts for our family and the cast."

Kai blew a kiss to her sister across the kitchen. "Axe and I appreciate that, Marina. That means a lot to the performers. We're putting up some at our house, and others are staying at the inn."

"Brooke, Chip, and the boys will take rooms here," Ginger said. "It's too far for them to drive so late."

Kai wagged a finger. "Don't forget little Clover in that bunch."

"It's almost like the old days again," Marina said.

She loved gathering with her family at Ginger's for Christmas morning, which was mainly for the little ones. She and Jack would exchange gifts at their home. This year, they'd agreed on modest presents.

When she and her sisters were younger, Ginger always had a houseful of people. Marina revived the tradition and took over the task after she returned to Summer Beach. They all loved opening the house to neighbors and friends.

"Now I have the luxury of all of you helping out," Ginger said, smiling. "Having a chef and talented sous chefs and bakers in the family is marvelous."

Marina put the cheesecakes into the hot oven and set the timer. "While these are baking, let's finish everything else so we can clean up and start our Christmas Eve festivities."

"Just a few more minutes for these," Kai said, sliding the last cookies into the other oven. "Then, I need to drop off Stella at the sitters. Axe and I planned to go to the Shell early to meet with the stage director about tonight's show."

"I'm sure the show will be spectacular," Ginger said. "And that goes for the feast, too."

Marina embraced her grandmother. "I know it will be. I learned from the best—from you."

AFTER CHANGING into a sparkly sweater and boots, Marina arrived at the outdoor amphitheater with Jack and Leo. They greeted friends as they made their way to their seats.

Her friends Ivy and Shelly called to them, "Merry Christmas Eve to you all."

"Merry Christmas," Marina said.

She loved this new tradition of gathering at the Shell, thanks to the vision and efforts of Kai and Axe. The holidays were a blend of old and new traditions now as their family was evolving.

While Leo ran ahead to see his friend Samantha, Marina and Jack stopped to speak to Imani Jones and her son, Jamir, who was attending medical school. Louise from the Laundry Basket and Rosa with her family were seated behind them.

They made their way to the section that Axe had reserved for them. Her daughter and her fiancé were already there.

"Hi, Mom. What do you think?" Heather and Blake wore matching Christmas sweaters.

"You two look adorable. Have you seen your brother?"

"There he is." Heather motioned to Ethan. "And look who is with him. Do you mind if Holly and Brandy join us afterward at the café?"

"I'd be delighted to have them."

"Good, because he already asked them. You know how Ethan is."

"Everyone is welcome." Marina smiled as she watched her son catering to Holly. He was introducing her to his friends. While it was far too soon to read anything into their budding relationship, Marina wondered if fate had more than one reason to bring Holly to Summer Beach.

Kai and Axe soon joined them, waving at friends along the way.

"It feels different being in the audience," Kai said, sitting beside Marina. She wore a showstopping red sequined top under a silver puffy jacket and gloves.

The retired nurse Marina knew had offered to look after her baby and Brooke's tonight to give the mothers a night off.

"Don't enjoy it too much," Jack said, grinning. "Everyone misses seeing you on stage this year."

"It won't be long unless Stella has a sibling," Kai said.

Marina's eyes widened. "What? Are you—"

Kai laughed and shook her head. "No, but we're not ruling out the possibility. I'm not going for Brooke's record, but we could manage one more."

"What about my record?" Brooke asked. She took a seat behind them with Chip and their three boys.

"Kai is thinking about playing catch-up in the family department."

"But not entirely," Kai added. "You have a head start, and I have limited patience."

Marina looked around. Everyone was there tonight—her sisters and their husbands and all their children.

"Hello, everyone," Ginger said, sitting with Oliver and

spreading thick blankets over their legs. Oliver had a pair of thermoses.

Marina smiled at her grandmother; she looked happy tonight, surrounded by family. She and Oliver held hands and bent their heads together, speaking softly.

Jack followed her line of sight. "Look how sweet they are with each other. They're like us—completely in love."

"They are, aren't they?"

Having been lucky enough to find love again herself, Marina could hardly begrudge Ginger a second chance. Oliver was a prince of a man whose manners and attitude were reminiscent of Bertrand. And he adored her just as much.

No wonder Ginger had fallen in love with him. Marina let out a sigh at the sudden thought.

Jack put his arm around her. "Are you okay?"

Marina whispered, "I've been thinking about Ginger and Oliver. I know what they're considering. They've led brilliant, adventurous lives and are still in excellent health. If they want to start their life together elsewhere, we should send them off with our best wishes." She must be prepared for the possibility.

"They would be deeply missed." Jack took her hand and kissed it. "But no one can predict the future. Let's just enjoy the holidays with them. This year will be one to remember."

"They all are," Marina said.

Just then, the lights flickered, indicating the show was about to begin.

12

*M*arina wrapped her jacket tighter around her shoulders as an ocean breeze swept through the venue. The aroma of hot cocoa and the sound of lively conversations filled the air.

All around her, the faces of her loved ones glowed in the light of thousands of twinkling bulbs. She tipped her head back, taking in the stars flickering above them.

"Beautiful, isn't it?" Jack squeezed Marina's hand, and she leaned into familiar warmth.

Soon, the stage lights illuminated the stage, and the audience applauded. A thrill of anticipation filled Marina.

The decorations were breathtaking—crystalline snowflakes suspended in mid-air, garlands of silver and gold draped elegantly across set pieces, and at stage right, an enormous Christmas tree decorated entirely in coastal themes: starfish, shells, and glass orbs in the colors of the sea.

Marina knew Kai had overseen the set design. She tapped her sister. "Everything looks gorgeous."

"Wait until you hear them," Kai replied.

They didn't have to wait long for the choir members to file onto the stage. The women wore floor-length, cranberry-red dresses, and the men sported matching bow ties with black suits.

The conductor strode onto the stage to thundering applause.

"Welcome to the Shell," the conductor said. "We hope you enjoy yourselves this evening as our award-winning Coastal Community Choir performs A Very Choral Christmas for you. Let's also honor one of our most beloved benefactors, Ginger Delavie."

Ginger looked pleasantly surprised, yet she stood and turned to wave as applause swept across the venue. "Thank you very much."

"I had no idea," Marina said to her sisters.

"None of us did," Brooke said. "But that's our grandmother."

As the choir launched into its opening medley, Marina let the familiar holiday music with a beach twist wash over her, lifting her spirits.

She smiled at the opening notes of "Deck the Palms," which swapped holly and ivy for seashells and starfish in the lyrics. The audience clapped along with "Jingle Shells," and seashell tambourines echoed through the night.

Everyone cheered at "I'm Dreaming of a Sunny Christmas." Their celebrations by the beach might not include snow or sleigh rides, but they still had love, family, and sunshine.

When soloist Allyson Chang stepped forward for her "Silent Night" solo, her crystal-clear soprano soaring into the sky, emotion overcame Marina. Tears pricked the corners of her eyes.

Jack pulled her closer and kissed her cheek. "That got me, too," he said, wiping his cheeks with a knuckle.

At intermission, the family stood to stretch their legs, and friends surrounded Ginger. Marina loved these moments with family, friends, and music under the stars.

Jack stood and rolled his shoulders. "Chip and I can bring drinks for everyone. How many hot cocoas and coffees do we need?"

"I'll help," Blake said, rising to his feet.

"And I need to check on things backstage," Axe said.

After the men left, Marina turned to Ginger. "What an incredible show. Everyone in the choir is so talented."

"They clearly love what they do," Ginger said. "That's the secret to life."

Kai leaned into the conversation. "Axe always loved singing with them. I still swoon over his rich baritone."

A thought came to Marina. "Do you think we might see him on the stage tonight?"

Kai shook her head. "He said they asked him to sing with them, but he didn't have time to rehearse because of that big job. I know he wanted to." She brightened. "But next year, we'll put on another musical. How about Sandy the Sandman? A beach relative of Frosty?"

Marina grinned. "That's close to 'Mr. Sandman,' isn't it?"

Kai snapped her fingers and hummed the tune. "You're right. We could play with that."

A young man with a blond ponytail approached them. "Hey, everyone," Cruise said. "There's such a long line that Jack asked me to bring the cocoa and coffee out."

"Where is he?" Marina asked.

"Men's room. Long line there, too." Cruise shrugged.

"That's a first," Kai said, raising her eyebrows.

Before long, the lights blinked, and Marina glanced around. Still, there was no sign of Jack. Blake and Chip were missing, too. She sighed. They would find their way back.

"Where are they?" Kai craned her neck, looking. "I'm disappointed they're not back yet," she whispered.

Onstage, the lights went up, and the music soared. Men in tuxedos stepped out from behind set pieces, singing "All I Want for Christmas is You."

"Oh, my gosh, it's Axe," Kai cried, clapping. "And there's Jack."

Marina gasped and nudged Ginger. "Oliver is up there, too."

Ginger laughed. "I think they all are. Even the boys."

Sure enough, Leo led Alder, Rowan, and Oakley onto the stage, and all the girls in the crowd screamed.

Marina and her sisters broke into laughter. "Do we have a new boy band in the making?"

"Maybe I should book them now," Kai said, clapping along.

"What a surprise," Marina said, blowing Jack a kiss. With love blooming in her heart, she thought about the time they must have devoted to practicing and the effort required to keep this a secret.

"I have a feeling Axe's client wasn't as demanding as I thought," Kai said happily.

Marina tapped Ginger on the shoulder. "Did you know about this?"

She shook her head. "I suspected something, but never this. Isn't it clever?"

Marina loved the performance, and each of the men pointed to their sweethearts on the song's last line.

The crowd exploded with applause, and the guys exited into the audience, beaming.

Marina threw her arms around Jack. "All I want is you, too."

"Surprised?" he asked.

"All of us were," she replied, laughing. "That meant so much to me." Marina kissed him and whispered, "I love you, sweetheart. Merry Christmas."

As Jack's lips warmed hers, she thought of the first time she'd seen him and how far they had come. While they couldn't know the future, she had faith that they would celebrate their lives surrounded by family and the warmest of love.

13

"Why don't you drive?" Ginger suggested as they strolled toward the parking area after the performance.

"Are you sure?" Oliver replied, putting his arm around her.

"Tonight I want an excuse to wrap my arms around you." She had something important to ask him.

Oliver threw his head back and laughed. "You never need an excuse for that—you always have my permission."

When they reached the scooter, Ginger slipped on her helmet, and he helped her onto the back of the Vespa.

After he got on, she slid her arms around his torso and squeezed.

"Ready back there?" he asked.

"I'm ready for anything." She flipped her red scarf over her shoulder as the scooter rumbled to life. "Let's take the beach route to the cafe. It's such a beautiful night."

"You read my mind." Oliver steered through the

parking area. "Do you think anyone will mind if we're a little late?"

Ginger laughed into the breeze. "One advantage to age is we can do as we please. Within reason," she added. "Merry Christmas," she called out, waving as they passed people she knew.

Friends answered her and waved them through the line of cars exiting.

"See? Age has its benefits," she said.

"No, that's all for you, darling." Oliver chuckled. "I feel like I'm with a celebrity. You're adored in Summer Beach. Will you miss that?"

"That was never a goal for me." She rested her head against his shoulder, enjoying the ride as they whizzed past a kaleidoscope of lights down Main Street. She could feel the beating of his heart, matching her own.

Within minutes, they were near the beach, and Oliver veered to one side. "Mind if we stop?"

"Let's. The moonlight on the waves is breathtaking." She removed her helmet and rested it on the scooter as he did the same.

They were alone on the beach. In the distance, the starry night sky kissed the sea on the horizon. Oliver reached for her hand, and they strolled toward the waves in lockstep as if they'd been doing this all their lives.

Pausing at the water's edge, Oliver turned to her. "I've been thinking...our life is what we decide to make of it."

"I've always thought so, too. There's something I want to talk to you about." She squeezed his hand. "We've both created the paths we wanted..."

"I've admired that about you." He brought her hand to his lips and kissed her fingers.

Ginger warmed to his touch. She selected her words carefully, though she wanted to appear nonchalant. "You were fabulous onstage tonight. What a marvelous surprise. You were so charming, distinguished, and handsome. I felt like the luckiest woman in the audience when you pointed to me."

"I meant every word of it. All I want for Christmas, and the rest of my life, is you." He dropped slowly to one knee. "Will you marry me, Ginger?"

"Oh, for heaven's sake," she said, pulling him to his feet. "You might hurt your knees on a shell or a piece of driftwood. Let's not end a romantic evening like that. What will I do with you?"

He laughed, shaking his head. "You can't answer a question like that with a question. It's not an answer."

"Of course it is. Let's be partners, Oliver. You know I won't have it any other way." She hesitated, but only for dramatic effect. She knew what she wanted, but he had beat her to the question. Still, she wanted it noted for the record. "My dearest Oliver, will you marry me? I had hoped to ask you first."

Smiling, he pressed a hand to his heart. "A million times, my love."

"That sounds rather extravagant," Ginger said. "Let's start with just once." She met his lips in a kiss that made her feel like a young woman again. Then, tapping her foot, she said, "Now, what shall we do about rings? Some traditions I'm all for."

Oliver slapped a hand to his cheek and shook his head with a merry expression. "You really are something. This isn't going quite like I envisioned. I thought we'd shop for rings together."

"Why, I like that idea even better. Not that I need one, but I wanted to chide you a little, so we don't get too serious about this. At our age, that could be dangerous."

"And riding a scooter isn't?"

"Not in Summer Beach. People watch out for celebrities."

Laughing, Oliver wrapped his arms around her. "Please don't ever change. You keep life interesting, Ginger Delavie."

"As do you, Oliver Powell. You know, I think we'll be fabulous together."

"We already are."

Ginger looped her red scarf around his neck and drew him in for a kiss.

In each other's arms, the years melted away. Their love, like nature, was timeless. Waves still raced to the shore, stars still glimmered in the sky, and the sun would rise again.

Ginger knew this was the right step for them. "Should we join the party now?"

"I'd like that. Do you want to share our news tonight?"

"I think it will make a marvelous memory, but are you ready for their questions about where we plan to live?"

Oliver raised his brow and nodded. "I've been pondering that, and tonight, I had an epiphany. I have a proposal for you."

"Another one?"

"There's always another option, my love."

They strolled back to the scooter, deep in conversation.

· · ·

By the time Ginger and Oliver arrived at the cafe, their family and friends were crowded around the firepit and lining up for the buffet Marina had organized.

"Over here," Marina called, motioning them to the chef's table in the kitchen area. "We saved seats for you."

She warmed food on the stovetop while Brooke ferried dishes to the buffet table. Ethan poured the wine, and Heather stirred hot cocoa.

"Why, thank you, dear. What a marvelous holiday party." Ginger loosened her scarf.

"Where have you been?" Kai asked, cradling a sleeping little Stella. "We were getting worried about you. We picked up the girls from the sitter and were surprised we beat you here."

Oliver put his arm around Ginger, his eyes twinkling. "Should we tell them?"

"Why not? It's Christmas Eve." Ginger beamed at her family and, taking Oliver's hand, said, "We stopped by the beach, and we proposed to each other."

"Oh, my goodness," Kai said, bouncing in her seat. "You're engaged?"

Oliver looked at Ginger with pride, and she nodded. "In the interest of time, we decided to skip an engagement and simply get married. We're considering New Year's Day because everyone will be here. We could invite the pastor to our open house for a brief ceremony before the feast."

Kai's eyes glittered. "That's fabulous. I'll help organize it."

"And where will you live?" Marina asked.

"We weighed our options," Ginger replied. She had told Oliver that Marina would probably be the first to ask the question. "We've come up with a brilliant idea."

Oliver cleared his throat. "My nephew wants me to move near him in Boston, but I can't take Ginger out of her element. I've also grown accustomed to Summer Beach and all of you, who have welcomed me into your family."

Marina smiled. "We love having you. You've made our grandmother so happy."

"Indeed he has." Ginger kissed Oliver's cheek. "He offered to build a new home for us here, one that would be ours together."

Oliver shook his head. "We decided we'd rather visit Paris and Marrakech than spend time doing that, especially since Ginger already has a home on the beach."

"However, I thought Oliver should feel like it's his home, too," Ginger said. "So we came up with a compromise."

"What's that?" Heather asked, setting two mugs of hot cocoa in front of them.

"Why, thank you," Oliver said, pausing for a sip. "We decided to add a large primary suite onto the lower level of the cottage. We might grow weary of stairs someday, and I want Ginger to have a luxurious whirlpool bath."

Ginger nudged him and smiled. "Large enough for two, I should think. For therapeutic reasons, of course."

Jack grinned. "Is that what you call it?"

While Marina swatted her husband, Oliver lifted his chin toward Axe. "What do you think about that idea? From a building perspective, can you make it work?"

"I'm sure we can," Axe replied. "It's a great solution."

"That's what we thought, too." Oliver squeezed Ginger's shoulder. "I'll sell my home, and we'll buy a town-home in Boston to visit Chris and his family."

"I've always loved Boston and Cambridge," Ginger

said. "We can take trains all over the East Coast, and it's a short flight to Europe from there."

A smile grew on Marina's face. "You've figured it out, haven't you?"

Kai looked relieved. "We were all so worried you'd move away and we'd never see you again. We still need you."

"None of you need me, but I'm flattered you think so," Ginger said, smoothing a hand over Kai's. "You're all marvelous young women—and men."

"I like this idea," Marina said.

Heather nodded, too. "I'll move out when Blake and I marry, so you'll have the cottage to yourselves." She paused, looking a little embarrassed. "If that's okay with you. Or I could move in with Mom, Jack, and Leo for a few months."

"No, dear," Ginger said. "We both want you to stay there."

Marina came around the table and hugged Ginger. "I'm so glad you and Oliver found a path ahead."

"Perhaps Holly's ornament foretold our future as well." Ginger smiled and said, "There is always a way to create the life you want." She looked around the table into the faces of those she loved. "That goes for every one of you."

"Hear, hear," Oliver said, raising his mug. "And here's to a Merry Christmas for all of us."

"And so much more," Ginger said. "May the warmth of this holiday season spill over into the new year and beyond."

As the clock struck midnight, they all clinked their mugs—to Christmas, the future, and a sunny life ahead.

AUTHOR'S NOTE

More to Enjoy

Thank you for reading the Coral Cottage series! Be sure to join my Readers Club to keep in touch and receive news on special events and sales at www.janmoran.com.

For more feel-good beach reads, check out my next series, starting with *Beach View Lane*, and meet the Raines family of Crown Island. April Raines dreams of starting a historical society on sunny Crown Island, and her two grown daughters also want to recast their lives. The buzz around the island is that Ryan Kingston, a mysterious investor, has purchased the historic Majestic Hotel. Can they all come to terms with the past to start fresh? If you're following the series, look for one of my latest, *Hibiscus Heights*, book #4.

If you haven't read the Seabreeze Inn at Summer Beach series, I invite you to meet art teacher Ivy Bay and her sister Shelly as they renovate a historic beach house in *Seabreeze Inn*, the first in the original Summer Beach series.

If you've followed the series, look for book #11, *Seabreeze Library*.

You might also enjoy more sunshine and international travel with a group of best friends in a series sprinkled with sunshine and second chances, beginning with *Flawless* and an exciting trip to Paris.

Finally, I invite you to read my *standalone historical novels*, including *Hepburn's Necklace* and *The Chocolatier*, a pair of 1950s sagas set in gorgeous Italy.

Most of my books are available in ebook, paperback or hardcover, audiobook, and large print on my shop and from all major retailers. And as always, I wish you happy reading!

PUMPKIN CHEESECAKE RECIPE

In *A Very Coral Christmas*, Marina's Pumpkin Cheesecake is a delicious twist on the classic cheesecake. This easy pumpkin cheesecake recipe is guaranteed to please. I've been making this recipe for my family for years.

I've also included baking tips I've learned to keep the top from cracking. Or add a dollop of cinnamon-spiced whipped cream over each slice to hide imperfections. I hope you'll savor this holiday cheesecake as much as my family does.

Ingredients:

Crust

1 cup (240 ml) of graham cracker crumbs
3/4 cup (180 ml) of ginger snaps
3 tablespoons (45 ml) brown sugar, light preferred
1 teaspoon (5 ml) ground cinnamon
1/2 teaspoon (2.5 ml)ground nutmeg

1/2 cup (1 stick) (120 ml or 113 g) of melted butter

Filling

24 ounces (680 g) of cream cheese (room temperature)
15 ounces (425 g) of pureed pumpkin
4 eggs (room temperature)
1/4 cup (60 ml) sour cream
1 1/3 cups (320 ml or 267 g) sugar
2 tablespoons (30 ml) flour
1 teaspoon (5 ml) ground cinnamon
1/2 teaspoon (2.5 ml) ground nutmeg
1/4 teaspoon (1.25 ml) ground cloves
1 teaspoon (5 ml) vanilla

Directions:

Crust

1. Preheat oven to 350 °F.

2. Crush graham crackers and ginger snap cookies. Mix in a medium bowl with sugar and spices. Melt butter and add. Press lightly into the bottom of a 9-inch springform pan. (Note: If pressed too firmly, the crust will be hard. If extra, bring it up the sides of the pan.)

Note: To avoid drips (butter may melt), place a cookie sheet of foil on a lower rack in the oven. You might also wrap the bottom of the pan with heavy tin foil. See the baking tips below on how to avoid cheesecake cracking.

Filling

1. Beat the cream cheese to a smooth consistency. Add eggs one at a time and blend, but do not overbeat. Add pureed pumpkin, sour cream, and vanilla. Mix in sugar, spices, and flour. Beat until smooth and well-blended. Pour into prepared crust.

2. Bake for 1 hour. The center will be slightly moist and nearly underdone. (Note: If too underdone, add up to 10 minutes, depending on your oven.) Crack open the oven and let cool in the oven for 15 minutes. Remove and let cool. Cover with plastic film and chill for 4 hours.

Baking Tips: Cheesecakes tend to crack in the dry heat of an oven. To avoid cheesecake cracking, let it remain in the oven after baking to cool down slowly.

Some like to press extra crust up the side of the pan, reasoning that it might ease the cooling contraction process.

Another method is to introduce more moisture into the oven through the use of a *bain-marie*, or water bath (placing the wrapped springform pan into a larger pan of hot water to bake). An easier method is to place a bowl of water in the oven to create moist heat.

ABOUT THE AUTHOR

JAN MORAN is a *USA Today* and a *Wall Street Journal* bestselling author of romantic women's fiction. A few of her favorite things include a fine cup of coffee, dark chocolate, fresh flowers, laughter, and music that touches her soul. She loves to travel to gain inspiration and meet readers. Jan is originally from Austin, Texas, and a trace of a drawl still survives, although she has lived in Southern California near the beach for years.

Most of her books are available as audiobooks, and many are translated into German, Italian, Polish, Dutch, Turkish, Russian, Bulgarian, Portuguese, and Lithuanian, among other languages.

If you enjoyed this book, please consider leaving a brief review online for your fellow readers where you purchased this book or on Goodreads or Bookbub.

To read Jan's other historical and contemporary novels, visit JanMoran.com. Join her VIP Readers Club mailing list and Facebook Readers Group to learn of new releases, sales and contests.

Made in United States
Cleveland, OH
09 June 2025

17617747R00069